Gama and Hest

A COMPANION STORY TO
THE AHSENTHE CYCLE

ALEXES RAZEVICH

ONE

Outside, the air grumbled and growled. Hest shot Gama a quick look, his eyebrow ridges hiked up, making small dark furrows on his forehead. Gama shrugged and continued the chant. The old ones said it never rained on Emergence Day, and it hadn't—not in her lifetime or the lifetimes of the oldest among them. Still, the rumble plucked at her nerves.

Steam filled the windowless room, condensing on Gama's skin, making it glisten. Tiny transparent crystals formed in the heat, sliding down so infinitesimally slowly it was like the movement of stars. The steam was for the three hatchlings gathered there with the adults, to soften their outer skins and make shedding it easier. Once the skin was sloughed off, a new adult would stand before them, ready to join the community.

Hest's skin was lighter than Gama's. The droplets didn't stand out against his face as brightly as those on her skin. He lifted a hand—his smaller one, meant for liberating the egg during mating—and wiped away the moisture that wet his face.

It was a nice face, Hest's. Gama had liked it when she first saw it at their own Emergence, when their downy outer coatings had been stripped away and they had discovered themselves as adult soumyo. He had light orange-red skin that contrasted sharply with his black eyes, a thin but attractive chest, and one hand small and delicate—the one he was now using to wipe his face now—and the other sturdy, with a fine digger claw for routing out a nest at mating time. They were about the same height, but her skin was a darker and clearer red, her eyes yellow, and her female hands a perfect if opposite match.

Someone put more wood on the fire below two large cauldrons filled with water, aromatic leaves, barks, and roots. Gama heard the crack and sizzle of the new wood being fed to the flames. Scents sweet, woody, and savory filled the air. Standing at the back of the large room, she couldn't see through her kin to know who had done it, though her guess would have been Prill, Reln's apprentice.

Hest gently elbowed her side and mouthed the word, *male*. Gama shook her head. They'd played this game last year, too—predicting what gender each hatchling would be when it emerged. He was terrible at it, guessing male nearly every time—hoping for more of his own kind, she supposed. She was better at the game, and felt sure this one would be female. It pleased her to think she'd soon have a new sister.

When she was right, Hest slumped—exaggerated for effect, as usual—against the wall: plaster over stone and wood, the plaster mixed with pulverized green rocks to give it a bright color. He sent a thought her way, the thought-grains traveling

4

silently across the short distance through the moist air: *You cheat, Gama.* Anyone looking at them would see the thought-grains moving, but by convention anyone who didn't receive the thought would ignore what they'd seen and not speculate on what was said.

She leaned next to him on the wall. It was impossible to cheat—no one could know a hatchling's gender in advance, though there were those who claimed to recognize the tiny signs of difference. Gama was wondering what those telltale signs might be when the world outside exploded.

A tremendous bang shook the room, louder than in the lightning storms last year that had lit the skies for days and brought thunder that made her ear holes ring. The wall they leaned against quivered, fear running through the structure the same as it ran through her.

"Out!" Reln, their guide, shouted and the structure threw open the door. Gama lunged toward the three new adults, their hatchling-down still lying at their feet, anxiety bright on their emotion spots. Before she covered four steps, Prill had reached the new adults and was leading them toward the door. Reln hastily put out the fires beneath the large cauldrons, smothering them with sand from the buckets kept full for that purpose. Hest grabbed Gama's hand, his digger claw a hard and comforting presence in her palm. She closed her fingers around it, holding tight.

Outside, everything looked the same— structures, dwellings, the commons, and the high wall around them, the parts of Reev she could see from where she stood. Nothing had collapsed or exploded. The sky was blue and cloudless. The heat on her emotion spots shifted as they changed from the blue-red of anxiety to the orange-yellow of confusion. The same colors showed on Hest's neck and on the throats of their sisters and brothers. Usually a harmony of feelings among her kin was a soothing sight. Now it bothered her, like having a stone in her foot casing but finding nothing there when she shook it out.

Hest nudged her and pointed up, out beyond Wall, above where the orchards they'd been harvesting stood. "Do you see that?"

She strained her eyes but saw only treetops and sky.

Above the trees, Hest thought-talked. *A sort of shimmer?*

Gama shaded her eyes with her hand and looked hard where he'd pointed, but didn't see anything unusual. Hest's lips pushed together in a line.

It was there, he sent.

She glanced at her sisters and brothers milling around them. They were nervous, disturbed, but none paid any attention to the sky. *It must have gone.*

Hest looked away, as though he couldn't bear it if she doubted him.

-=o=-

The second bang came in the night. Females and males poured from their dwellings, some hastily tying on hip wraps or throwing on cloaks, but most running without dressing, too panicked to even pull on foot casings to protect their feet.

Gama and Hest ran outside together, Home sending behind them, *What's happening? What's happening?* Gama shook her head, though she never knew how much structures could read gestures.

Their brothers and sisters filled the commons, everyone as confused as they were, some talking to the kin next to them, but most standing open-mouthed, glancing wildly in every direction, their necks aflame in the gray-red of shock or the muddy-brown of fear.

Another huge boom cut the air. Hest grabbed Gama's arm with his soft hand and pointed into the night sky with the other. Above them, off to the left, the air shimmered like sunlight on still water. Gama's heart beat fast. The frightened structures called to each other, all talking at once in their own speech that sounded like a long blow of wind. She leaned close to Hest, for the comfort of his skin.

"Look!" a sister called, her eyes on the sky.

A disk-shaped swath of stars went out—not one by one, but all at once, as though the sky had swallowed them whole. *We should go. We should go*, the structures sent in words Gama could understand. Wall flapped its five wooden gates open and shut, open and shut, as if desperate to get Reln's attention, since only he could make the decision for the corenta to move.

Gama grabbed Hest's hand and pulled him with her as she ran through the crowd toward their guide, ducking around their sisters and brothers. Reln stood transfixed, his head tilted back, his mouth hanging open. Gama grabbed his shoulders and shook them.

"You see that?" Reln stared hard at the sky.

Above their heads, burning blue flames filled a starless circle in the night sky. Gama stared as the circle grew, the licking flames filling in where stars had been. She stared so long and hard her eyes watered. She tightened her hold on Hest's hand.

Another boom rang out.

Behind it, low and deep—a hum.

And then the flames were gone, flicked out like covering a candle, the black circle of sky once again filled with stars.

Reln shut his mouth and dropped his chin, his gaze moving from face to face. Everyone waited for him to speak.

"Return to your dwellings," he said, raising his voice to be heard. "It's over now."

They turned slowly, the two hundred and fourteen sisters and brothers of Reev corenta, some confused, some frightened—everyone grabbing onto Reln's words and the calm, sure way he'd said them, as if he had a secret knowledge and they could trust those words completely.

Gama let loose of Hest and rubbed her hands over her thighs. It didn't feel over to her. It felt dangerous.

Two

The hatchling pair carried one bucket between them, the silver-gray pail swinging from their hands like a broken gate. The pair followed Hest toward the river as though he led them on a string. Gama brought up the rear. Three days had passed since the shimmering sky and the swallowed stars. Nothing odd had happened since, but still she half-listened for the hum.

Reln and his apprentice, Prill, had walked out of Reev with her and Hest, but had gone the other direction in search of healing plants and soils. Prill came from the same mating grounds as she did. Gama felt sympathy for her, knowing Prill didn't like being outside of Reev's protective wall, but didn't truly understand her feeling. She loved Reev and the open spaces both.

Gama smiled, watching the hatchlings mimic Hest's every move. These two hatchlings were off-Resonance young, not hatched the year their egg was laid, but developing more slowly. She and Hest had been off-Resonance hatchlings themselves, and she felt a special kinship with them.

An image formed in her mind—two happy hatchlings sitting with their feet dangling in the water. Hatchlings didn't get full language abilities until they emerged and they could be a bit like plants at times, sending thought-pictures that needed deciphering, but this one was easy enough to figure out.

Gama laughed. "It has been a long walk. This is a good spot. Set down your bucket and we'll show you how to find nokifs. You like nokifs, don't you?"

The hatchlings nodded their enthusiasm for the fist-sized purple-red bulbs that while bitter-tasting fresh from the plant were soft and delicious boiled. The stiff stems with feathery fronds weren't good for eating, but the bulbs were worth the work it took to harvest and prepare them.

Gama and Hest waded into the shallow water at the river's bank, their knives pulled from the tools belts at their waists and ready in their hands. A few small black-and-tan nibblers banged at Gama's ankles. She shook her foot to shoo them away.

"Nibblers?" Hest said.

"Greedy little beastlets. Always looking for an easy meal and not concerned about what gets in their way—especially when it's me. I don't see them banging around your legs."

Nokif stems and fronds were a favorite food of the nibblers, often gnawed down to the mud line by their sharp teeth. Nokif bulbs were easier to harvest if the stems were long. They could pull them up instead of having to dig them out. She'd had the idea to build woven walls in the river at the top and bottom of the stretch their corenta harvested. The wall would let water move freely, but keep new nibblers out and the trapped ones could be moved elsewhere. Over time, the nibblers would be less and the nokif more—at least it seemed that way to her. Reln was still thinking her idea over. Sometimes their guide thought a suggestion over a very long time before reaching a decision.

And sometimes—like with the disappearing stars—Reln decided a bit too quickly for Gama's liking that things were fine.

"Listen," Gama told the hatchlings. "We sing this request for permission before any harvest begins."

She sang *The Song of Sharing* to the nokif, acknowledging how intertwined they were and how they helped each other to survive. Hest hummed a harmony. Reln often said that she was the structure and Hest the embellishment, and between them they made a strong beauty. It was true that she and Hest seemed to bring out the best in the other. Prill had once remarked that Gama and Hest were so close they might as well have been hatched from the same egg. Gama liked the idea that she and Hest were each other's completing half. What better friendship could there be than that?

When she finished singing, she sent the nokif a quick picture of the woven wall that could spare them being eaten by nibblers—it never hurt to let food know you appreciated it and watched out for its welfare.

Gama and Hest held up their knives for the hatchlings to see, then beckoned them to come closer. The young ones sat on their heels at the riverbank's edge and watched Gama and Hest dig into the mud, twisting their knife blades to loosen and lift the bulbs, exaggerating their motions so the hatchlings could understand. They sent the hatchlings thought-pictures of what was happening beneath the mud—showing how the blade knocked a little when it hit the side of the bulb, how they twisted the blade down to find the bottom and then slid it underneath to work the bulb free.

The hatchlings watched intently as Gama and Hest dug dozens of bulbs, until one stood up and loudly said, "Us."

Hest smiled and handed his blade to the bold one. Gama gave her knife to its shyer nest-mate. They jumped into the river, their yellow down fluffing in the cold water to keep them warm, and began digging furiously. Hest sent Gama a look and she knew they were thinking the same thought— that teaching hatchlings was a particular joy. The two of them were almost always in harmony of thought and feeling, not something she could say about her and the rest of their kin. She reached out and stroked his wet neck in appreciation.

By day's end, they'd filled the three buckets to the top with nokif bulbs. The hatchlings' bucket was too heavy for them now, so Gama or Hest would carry it back to Reev. First though, all that hard work deserved immediate reward.

Hest took the bold hatchling by the hand. "I'll show you how to float in deep water."

Gama turned and gently splashed the shyer one. "You don't want to miss out on this." She sent a thought-picture of floating on her back, and grinned. "Come on. It's fun."

-=o=-

The sun had nearly set, the sky already turning gray when they hauled their happy, tired selves back onto the bank. The hatchlings wriggled all over, giggling as drops flew from their down. Hest sluiced water off his body with his digger hand and took up his bucket. Gama took up hers and looked for the hatchlings' bucket, but it wasn't there. She shot Hest a puzzled glance.

It has to be here, he sent. *No thief-beast came while we were in the water.*

I know. Gama poked among the reeds that grew on the bank, though she was sure she'd left the bucket in plain sight next to her own. *Maybe Reln and Prill came by and took it?*

I doubt it, Hest sent. *They had a long way to go in the opposite direction. Why walk all the way here just to take one bucket without telling someone?*

Then it has to be here. Gama rubbed the side of her mouth. *But it isn't.*

The shy hatchling sat down and mewled. Gama put her hand on its shoulder. "It's not your fault. You didn't lose the bucket. It's just misplaced. Let's walk down the bank a bit, see if it's there."

It was full dark when they gave up and headed back to Reev with two buckets of bulbs and a weight of confusion between them.

-=o=-

The flying beast flapped its big triangular red and

brown wings in the bright sun outside their window. The sight cheered her. It was good to see both the beast and the sun after several days when cloud cover had kept the days unusually cool and gloomy for the season. Gama nudged Hest and pointed with her chin so he'd see.

"A flying beast alongside a corenta is good luck," Hest said.

Gama didn't believe much in luck. Thorough preparation and hard work made good things happen. There was something cheerful about beasts scudding along next to Reev, though—sharing the same sky for that brief moment, or for as long as it rode the currents Reev set up in its flight.

"How far do you think it is to the next landing spot?"

"Far enough that I wouldn't want to have to walk it," Hest said.

Gama rolled her eyes. "There must have been a time when soumyo did walk. Corentas are built. So sometime in the way long ago, before the soumyo made the first corenta and it learned to fly, they must have walked from orchard to river to field to get what they needed."

Hest made a great show of examining the soles of his foot casings. "Good thing there are corentas now, then."

She laughed under her breath, glad for the diversion of conversation and for the pleasure of Hest's company. Being stuck inside a dwelling during travel let her mind wander to things it was probably better not to think about—like the bangs and the burning sky. Like a bucket of nokif that couldn't be found.

Hest. Do you think the bucket is still there, by the river?

"I asked around," he said aloud. "After we came back to Reev. No one had come by the river and taken a bucket, so I suppose it has to still be there."

She was sure she'd set that bucket down next to her own. How could she be so wrong?

"I feel bad that we lost it," she said. "The hatchlings blamed themselves, but it wasn't their work to keep track of it—it was ours."

Reev slowed its flight, preparing to land. She got up and went to the window to watch their descent. The flying beast weaved away to wherever it was going.

"You're thinking too much again," Hest said. "Probably the bucket fell in the river and the current carried it off."

She looked at him over her shoulder. "Do you really think that happened?"

"It could have. You might have left the bucket too close to the water. A beast came along and knocked it into the stream while we were floating in the water with the hatchlings. It's the only thing that makes sense."

She turned back to the window and thought that over, trying to remember exactly where she'd left the third bucket. She could have left it close to the water. She didn't think she had, but maybe.

There was a slight jolt as Reev bumped lightly against the soil, and then settled gently on the plain. Wall and the structures started speaking among each other in their own language. Gama looked out the window and waited for Home to get around to translating.

Impatience got the better of her. *What's going on?*

Someone has taken the grain, Home sent.

A nervous chill raced up her breastbone. *What do you mean?*

Wall says the plain is empty. Already harvested.

Gama pressed up against the window, trying to see, but Wall was in the way. An empty plain wasn't possible. Corentas traveled freely over the world, but each had claimed areas, sections of plains where wild grains grew, or a copse of trees with edible fruits, bark, or leaves, or a section of river, from which no other corenta would harvest. That way each community had what it needed with no need to argue over access. Claimed areas were clearly marked. Gama couldn't imagine another corenta taking grain from a field not their own.

Oh! Oh! Oh! Home sent. *Go see!*

Gama cleared the door first, Hest following. All the soumyo of Reev seemed to be rushing through the meandering paths toward the gates as though carried on a swift current. Someone ran by, knocking into Gama. She stumbled but Hest steadied her. More of their kin pushed by. Those who'd gotten through the main gate first stood only a little ways into the field. Gama and Hest could see them up ahead—all of them motionless. Hest angled through the standing soumyo to the front of the pack, clearing a path for her. A bead of sweat slid down the side of Gama's face.

No beasts or bugs had done this. No soumyo either. The grain hadn't been harvested or eaten. It was simply gone—the dry, brown soil bare of the slightest sign that anything had ever grown there, not just in their area, but across the entire valley. At least five other corentas would find their fields stripped.

Gama rubbed her hands on her thighs. This couldn't happen, but it had.

The corenta kin murmured among themselves.

Prill, who stood on the other side of Hest, said to no one in particular, "Wind? Could a wind blow hard enough to pull up every plant from its roots and scatter it someplace else?"

"There's no disturbances in the soil," Gama said, answering her. "If a wind ripped them up, the ground would show it."

Prill nodded and fell silent, as though her one idea had been hard enough, and she couldn't summon another.

Gama couldn't summon any ideas either. First the bangs, then the bucket, and now this. She stared out over the brown dirt of the valley, her mind numbed, her stomach in knots.

What do you see? Home sent with a sudden urgency that reminded her that of all the structures, only Wall saw what was outside.

Nothing, she sent. *Nothing but dirt.*

THREE

There was no point staying where they were, Reln had said. He'd sent everyone back to their dwellings while they moved again. Home had grumbled that Reln should have thought it through more, talked it through with the soumyo and structures, but Gama had just shrugged. That was Reln—taking too much time to reach a simple decision, and sometimes making major decisions in a rush. It was fine with her that they hadn't stayed at the barren plain. There was nothing there for them now. Besides, the further they traveled from the place of the burning sky, the better she felt. They were a long way from it now.

Truth was, she preferred the work where they were now. Instead of harvesting grain, as she would have at the fields, she and Hest hauled salt blocks out to the meadow near where Reev had set down. She liked the feel of the soft rope that encircled both their waists, the weight of the sled behind them, the effort it took to move it. She was stronger, but he pulled ahead and looked over his shoulder.

"Keep up, Gama, will you?"

She grabbed the rope between her hands and ran. She shouldn't have laughed, but Hest looked silly, stumbling, trying to keep up as they raced across the meadow. Delicate new pink shoots of whiltsprout tickled the bottoms of their bare feet. She could outrun him on one leg. She thought he'd have known that by now.

He was panting hard by the time they reached the meadow and the soft rise where they always brought the salt.

"Need a moment to catch your breath before we unload?"

Hest glowered at her, but was still breathing too hard to answer.

"Guess I'll get started by myself then." Gama pushed at a block on the sled. The blocks were big and heavy. It took two soumyo to move them, and she knew she couldn't push one off herself. Still, she exaggerated how hard it was, huffing and puffing, then standing up and wiping imaginary sweat from her brow.

Hest laughed softly once he had his breath back, and bent to help. Together they pushed the block, and shared the satisfaction of tipping it off the sled and onto the ground. They moved the sled a few feet and shoved another block off, then moved again, until all six blocks lay crushing the delicate shoots beneath them. The only thing left on the sled was the gathering bag that had been under the salt blocks.

Hest threw back his head, closed his eyes and trilled his tongue across the top of his mouth to make the sound that called the brez down to the salt.

She listened, thinking she liked the word brez—

the way it sounded in her mind and in the saying; that it was both singular and plural. One beast was brez. A large herd was brez. Soumyo was the same: one soumyo walked through Reeve, five soumyo followed.

Gama shaded her eyes and looked toward the low hills beyond the long, wide meadow. The soumyo of Reev had been coming to this meadow long enough that the brez who foraged there knew what Hest's call meant. She watched them come, four legged beasts as high at the shoulder as she was, their large, shaggy heads swaying slowly back and forth as they walked, their long, stiff tails moving in counterpoint behind them. Brez could move quickly when they wanted, but didn't often seem to feel much reason to. She wished they'd hurry; restless energy ran through her and she needed work to do.

She and Hest settled on a flat spot on the generally bumpy land and waited. Gama drummed her fingers against her thighs. Why were the brez so slow today? She took a deep breath and stilled her hands, willing herself to a calmness she couldn't quite reach.

Hest spotted something in the whiltsprout and bent to pick it up—a long thin piece of bone. Bird leg, from the shape. He wiped the top of the bone clean with his hipwrap and blew across the open tip to produce a high, breathy tone.

She nodded, glad for the diversion. Hest drew a deep breath and huffed air across the bone in a quick tempo, moving the bone around beneath his lips to change the sound. Gama smiled. Everyone liked music, but for Hest it was like a second heartbeat. She clapped her hands against her thighs in rhythm, in support more than enjoyment today. She suspected Hest was looking for distraction every bit as hard as she was, to avoid thinking about the explosion-sounds, the missing bucket the field wiped clean. Hest didn't want to talk about it. Even Reln had brushed off her tentative questions. There seemed to be an unspoken pact not to speak about these things—to not even think about them. As if silence could undo their fears.

It might have been better if they had talked. No one could *not* think about it. There was falseness to their joy now, and yet she pretended as hard as Hest did.

The brez must have found the music pleasing. They picked up their pace toward the salt licks. Hest blew across the bone. Gama clapped. The brez stopped and looked down at them, their moist blue eyes, the color of sky, and made their low ooooo-ya-oooo call. Hest put down the bone and the brez started in on the salt.

When the beasts had had their fill, they walked over to Gama and Hest, understanding that everything must be fairly traded, and that the soumyo got brez hair in exchange for the salt.

Hest opened a small bag hanging from the tools belt around his waist and drew out two combs. The brez stood placidly as the soumyo combed the beasts' long hair. Gama thought they liked it, which made it a perfect trade—the brez getting two things they enjoyed in exchange for the beasts' long, soft hair, which the soumyo wove into cloaks and blankets.

"Do you suppose brez think we come here in service to them?" Gama pulled hair from the filled comb and stuffed it into the bag.

Hest half shrugged. "Probably. We bring them salt. We groom them, which they like."

She ran her hand over her scalp. "It seems strange we don't have hair, or fur, or something to keep us warm. Hatchlings do, but when we emerge we're without anything to protect us. Seems like poor planning."

Hest rolled his eyes. "Always with the questions and opinions, Gama. All right, here's a reason. Because we *are* in service to the brez. If we could stay warm on our own, we wouldn't need their hair and wouldn't bring them salt." He held out his arm and made a show of looking at it. "Besides, it would be a shame to mar this lovely skin of mine with hair or fur that hid it."

Gama laughed and returned to grooming the brez, working from the bottom of a tangle upward, to free the knotted hair. The beast under Gama's hands closed its large blue eyes and muttered contently in its own language. She couldn't understand the speech but saw its happiness in her mind—a slowly rotating, bright silver ball.

Other beasts had different images for their emotions. Some projected a screen of green or other color so large it took up their whole mind. Others saw members of their own kind, sometimes pressed up against their flanks or nuzzling at the neck.

Gama fell into the beast's pleasure, felt its happiness as her own happiness and contentment as she ran the comb gently through the long variegated hairs—black, brown, and light gray—until the comb was full. It took a lot of strokes to fill the comb, and a lot of packed combs to stuff the bag. The sun was sinking by time they were done.

She finished with the last brez and lost the contentment connection. Thoughts of the explosion flowed back into her mind. The lost bucket. The field stripped clean. She shifted from foot to foot.

Don't think about it, Hest sent.

Of course he knew exactly what gnawed at her.

You're not thinking about it? It's scratching at my thoughts like a bird in a box.

He sighed. "We have work to do, Gama."

More brez had come to the salt patch than they had time to groom, and those who'd not gotten their chance at the comb now pawed the ground and snorted their displeasure.

We'll be back tomorrow. Gama didn't think the beasts understood the words, but knew from experience they understood the meaning.

But the beasts didn't settle.

The ones they'd groomed also started bellowing and pawing the ground. One nearly stomped on Hest's foot. He yelled, and jumped to get out of the way. Gama grabbed his arm and tugged him toward her. The beasts turned and sprang across the meadow toward the low hills that bordered it.

Hest!

"I don't know what scared them," he said aloud, knowing, as usual, what she was thinking as they watched the last of the beasts retreat—a female and an offspring. He shrugged uneasily. "At least we filled the bag."

Gama glanced at the stuffed-full bag, then back toward where the beasts had run. She and Hest had been grooming brez together since they'd emerged seven years earlier. They had a knack for it. Other pairs had to chase after the beasts and beg them to cooperate. Hest had been able to call brez from the start and both of them groomed the beasts practically without effort. Gama had never seen brez act the way these had. Unease churned in her belly. She tilted her head, thinking she heard a soft hum in the distance.

"Gama!" Hest said and grabbed her arm. He pointed toward the sky. "Do you see that?"

She looked up from where she was tying the bag onto the sled. A shiver ran up her breastbone. The air seemed to shimmer, the way Hest had said it had the day of the big booms.

"Let's go," she said, and sent, *Before the air explodes again.*

They grabbed the sled's rope and ran.

-=o=-

"Hest and Gama had a strange experience today. I wanted you to hear from them directly." Reln stretched out his hand, inviting Gama and Hest to stand beside him on the dais. Gama's neck warmed as she climbed the short stairway. She hated having attention focused her way. She liked even less knowing that what Hest and she had to say wasn't going to make their kin happy.

"I'll tell it if you want," Hest whispered as they took their places next to Reln. He switched to private thought-talk. Everyone in the room saw the thought-grains moving between them, but politely ignored them. *It's only two things: the brez were frightened and the shimmering sky. It's a quick story.*

She shot him a look of gratitude.

Below them the soumyo sat on pillows in the large open space of Community Hall. Reln stepped back, leaving her feeling alone on the dais, even with Hest beside her.

Hest cleared his throat and began the story. He told it well, straightforward, nothing extra, the way she remembered it. Not everyone recalled shared experiences in the same way, but Hest and she did. Gama panned her gaze across her brothers and sisters to gauge how they were taking the news. She picked out those who would have questions—the ones with real curiosity or worry showing on their throats, the ones who craved being the center of attention even for a brief moment, and those with the soft yellow-green of skepticism on their necks.

When Hest finished, Reln leaned forward, his long fingers splayed along his thighs—his standard thinking posture. He didn't speak. Gama wanted to flee the dais and sit with her corenta-kin, but courtesy was that a speaker stay put until all questions had been asked and answered. She looked across the room again, waiting.

Reln cleared his throat. "The shimmering sky is worrisome, but skittish brez are hardly reason to leave the area while we still have orchards to harvest, herbs to gather, and beasts to groom for this Barren Season's cloaks. Staying is even more important now. We must make up for the loss of the grain field that was destroyed."

Gama saw the colors playing across the throats of her kin as they listened—shades showing anxiety or resignation. She felt conflicted herself. Reln was right—they couldn't go flying off just because of one odd happening. But it wasn't only one event—it was one more.

"Our plan," Reln said, "is to remain here the next ten-day. I see no reason to change that. All of you will watch the sky and report anything unusual you see." He stepped down from the dais—a clear sign that no questions were to be asked, no other opinions were to be voiced.

A few of her sisters and brothers murmured to themselves or their neighbors, but most got up and walked toward the doors. The structures had all listened, and none spoke up—not even Hall, who usually felt the need to say something about any meeting held within its embrace. Gama clasped her hands together in front of her. There should have been discussion. She wasn't the only nervous soumyo in the room. But maybe Reln was right. Talk would only get the kin worked up. Better to keep busy. Better not to think too much about it.

The brownish-pink of uncertainty glowed softly on Hest's throat. She knew the same color showed on hers.

-=o=-

Kroot, kroot, Home sent, to get their attention. *Prill is coming.*

Gama looked up from where she sat on the floor weaving new fibers into her tools belt, strengthening it. *Welcome her, please.* Home opened its door wide.

Prill settled on the floor pillow next to Hest but turned her face to Gama. "Reln sent me. He saw you were worried at the end of the meeting. He wanted to know what bothered you."

Only one spot barely lit brownish-pink showed Prill's uncertainty and discomfort at having been sent to ask questions. But the heaviness Gama always felt from Prill was there—as though Prill lived her life carrying a large bag of sand in her arms.

Maybe that brownish-pink spot meant something else though. Maybe Prill thought the same as Gama did—that if Reln wanted answers, he could come ask for himself. Gama hoped so. She and Prill shared harmony of thought and feeling so rarely, it would be nice if they were together on this.

"The brez," Gama said. "They've never acted like that. And the shimmer we saw. What is that? Did the shimmer scare the beasts?"

Prill nodded, though Gama knew it wasn't in response to her questions. Two more spots lit on Prill's throat, light-gray joining brownish-pink.

What worried her? Prill always seemed to be holding back her thoughts, her desires. It drove Gamma mad that Prill didn't just say what was on her mind—spit it out and be done with it.

"Are you frightened, too, Prill?"

Prill huffed out a breath. More spots lit with discomfort colors. It took her a long moment to speak.

"Reln wants to gather herbs again tomorrow. He says it's up to us to show our sisters and brothers there's nothing to be worried about. That everything goes on as always."

Gama nodded. "What worries you about that?"

Prill scratched nervously at her leg but kept silent.

Gama already knew the answer. "You don't like being the healer's student, do you?"

Prill looked down at the floor. Her throat flared orange from embarrassment. "I don't like going outside Reev to gather herbs. I feel better inside. Safer. I don't like worrying all the time that I'll make a mistake, choose something that looks healing but is poisonous. Reln says he'll never push me to do anything I'm not ready for, but he wants me to start treating soon. That's worse than gathering. What if I give someone the wrong medicine and harm my corenta-kin?"

Usually females and males did a bit of every kind of work the first few years after emerging, then settled into what they liked or did best. Reln had taken Prill as his student almost as soon as she'd emerged. She'd never had a chance at anything else.

"Do you know why Reln chose you?"

She shook her head. "I've wanted to know, but I can't insult him like that. It's practically the same as saying he made a mistake. It would throw us out of harmony."

Hest, who'd sat quietly until now, said, "Seems like the two of you aren't in harmony anyway."

Prill's neck broke out in a mass of purple-gray and some blue-black spots. "We will be. I'll make sure of that."

Hest smiled kindly. "By finding the bits of the work that you enjoy."

Prill nodded. "There are parts I like, parts I'm good at. I have to pay attention to them and not to what frightens me."

Prill clasped her hands together in her lap. Hest caught Gama's eyes and rolled his own.

Gama half shrugged, leaned forward and touched Prill's neck. "What else bothers you?"

Prill opened her mouth and sucked in a large breath. When she spoke, the words rushed out. "These things that are happening. The stars that disappeared and then came back. Reln says not to worry about the nervous brez, but brez never get skittish. We even say 'happy as a brez' when someone is totally contented." She stopped suddenly. Her gaze darted between Gama and Hest, then dropped to her hands, still squeezed together in her lap. Her voice dropped to a near whisper. "Reln is making a mistake. It isn't safe here. We should go."

-=o=-

The already-loaded sled waited for them outside the storage room. Hest took his place inside the rope ring.

"Only four salt blocks today." Gama stepped in beside him and grabbed the rope with both hands, determined to be fearless. "Come on now, pull."

The day was warm and pleasant. Soft-bodied insects with whirring, fluttering wings flew past as Gama and Hest dragged the sled across Reev toward the gate. Gama tried to let the beauty of the day keep away her worries, but they slithered back.

"Hest, what do you think happened yesterday at the meadow?"

He hiked up his shoulders in a shrug. "I don't know. We saw the sky shimmer, but no bang followed, so maybe it was nothing. A natural happening we'd not noticed before."

"You'd think someone would have long since mentioned a shimmering sky, if they'd seen one."

Hest leaned forward, straining against the rope, putting his whole weight into pulling the sled. "We see the entire sky turn purple from time to time, but we don't run around telling everyone and pointing up."

"But the shimmer came before the boom. The boom wasn't anything normal."

"Maybe the boom and the shimmer have nothing to do with each other," he said.

She gave him a harsh look.

"You're always sure of everything, Gama. It still doesn't make it true."

"I'm not always sure, but when I am, I'm usually

right."

Hest rolled his eyes—as close as he was going to come to admitting the truth of that to her face.

They'd reached Wall, and waited as it opened its main gate to let them pass.

What do you say? Gama sent. *Does the sky shimmer from time to time? Do you see it so often you don't remark on it?*

The gate shut slowly behind them. She stopped and looked back.

The sky never shimmered that I recall, Wall sent. *And my memory is very long.*

"Still doesn't mean it has anything to do with the boom," Hest said aloud.

Gama frowned at him. They trudged across the meadow in silence. Trying to make sense of the strange occurrences of the last days was like trying to catch the wind in her hands.

"Maybe I misplaced the bucket that day by the river," she said finally. "Maybe a beast did knock it into the stream, but what about the field stripped of every living thing? You can't think that has nothing to do with anything else?"

"Coincidence," he said, and stopped. He wiped his brow with his soft hand.

Gama tightened her grip on the rope. "Because you want it to be."

"Coincidence because it is. I hope it is." He took the rope in his hands again and pushed forward. "We can't really dwell on it, can we? We need brez hair and there's only one way to get it. Let's go."

The meadow they were assigned was smaller

than yesterday's and lay in the shadow of the foothills. They pushed three salt blocks off the sled onto nearly bare ground that still waited for enough sunlight for whiltsprout to grow. Gama wished they had more blocks. Heavier blocks. Blocks she could strain against and yell with triumph over when she'd pushed them down.

"Do you want to try again to learn how to call the beasts?" Hest said as they shoved the last block onto the meadow.

She narrowed her eyes. "You're trying to distract my thoughts."

"Of course," he said. "And hoping you'll let me. Come on, give it a try."

She drew in a breath and held it while she decided he was right—it was foolish to cling to worry. Gama let the air go in a rush. "All right, but I don't think I'll get it."

"I think you will. You've been getting close the last couple of tries."

He'd been trying to teach her to call the brez for a while, but good as she was at some things, she was a failure at this, despite his patient efforts. "You go first."

Hest smiled, clearly pleased. "It's simple, really. The trick is to place your tongue at the right spot against the roof of your mouth. You keep putting your tongue too far forward. You want it behind your teeth."

Even though she'd just told him to go first, Gama tilted her head back, placed her tongue just behind her teeth and trilled.

Hest burst out laughing. "You sound like the wings of whirring insects, if they were as big as your head instead of the size of your smallest finger."

She felt her neck warm, and knew the blue-black of determination glowed on several of her spots. She leaned back her head and tried again.

The sound was perfect—an exact duplicate of the one Hest made. Gama cupped her palms against her thighs in celebration. Her emotion spots flared white with satisfaction. Hest stroked her neck.

"Did it work? What do you think?"

A low hum vibrated in the background—not like the hum she'd heard before the boom. This was different, higher pitched, nothing to worry about. Gama glanced around looking for whatever insects might be causing it, but couldn't see any.

Hest stared past her and said, "You did pretty good."

Gama followed his line of sight and saw a small herd of brez—maybe seven or eight strong—trotting down from the foothills toward them. Their hair, even at this distance, looked long, thick, and full. They'd have their bag filled in no time.

And then, as they watched, the brez vanished.

Four

The dais in Community Hall felt cold under Gama's foot casings, though she knew it wasn't really chilled—it was her own shaky nerves that made it feel that way. She looked out over the heads of their corenta-kin, glad that once again Hest was telling this news, not her. Their sisters and brothers held his face in their gaze so tightly she wondered if he felt it like a physical touch.

"One moment we were watching the brez come across the meadow to get the salt. The next moment," he clapped his cupped palm against his thigh "they were gone. We'd seen them on the hillside coming toward us. A small herd, maybe eight or nine. Gama called them." He glanced at her and touched the back of her arm with his soft hand. "They were coming, and then they weren't there at all."

The corenta-kin murmured among themselves, some turning to their neighbors now, eyes wide, and some shifting their gaze away—but some staring at Hest as if afraid to let go. The colors on their necks ran from the blue-red of anxiety to the greenish-orange of amazement. Here and there she caught sight of the gray-green of revulsion.

Reln rubbed his hand hard across his chin. "How

could they be gone?"

"I don't know." Gama stood between Hest and Reln on the dais and wished she were somewhere else—anywhere else. She wished she hadn't seen what she had, and didn't have to tell it to her sisters and brothers. Most of all, she wished these strange things weren't happening at all. "It was as if they were swallowed by the air."

"It wasn't a trick of the light?" Reln asked. "Perhaps the brez were spooked and turned back, and you misinterpreted what you thought you saw. You did say the beasts were a distance away."

Gama shook her head.

Hest blew out a quick breath. "They vanished. They were there, and they disappeared."

"Maybe gone with the grain in the bare field," she muttered, then covered her mouth with her hand, wishing she could stuff the words back in. Still, Gama felt sure there was a connection. It was as tangible as a sip of cool water in a parched mouth—as slippery as the last wisps of a fading memory.

Reln was quiet a long moment. If he'd heard her, he was willing to let the words go by without comment. She found Prill's face among the kin and focused on it instead. Prill's throat glowed with the colors of worry and insecurity; her hands were clasped tight together in her lap. Du sat next to Prill and leaned close, their shoulders touching. They were in tight harmony, the same colors alight on their throats in the same patterns.

"Did the sky shimmer before this happened?"

Reln asked, looking directly at her.

"Not that we saw. Though—"

Gama tried to see the moment again in her memory, tell it exactly as it happened. "I can't be sure, but maybe the air shimmered a little when the brez disappeared. I know the air felt funny—thick and heavy. I heard a humming sound before it happened."

Reln turned to Hest. "Did you see that, too? Feel that? Hear that?"

Hest shook his head. "No, but it was just as I said—one moment the beast were coming toward us; the next, it was as though they'd never been there at all."

Reln leaned forward and splayed his fingers on his thighs. "Vonti, would you stand please?"

Vonti pulled himself to his feet from where he'd been sitting. He was tall, probably the tallest among them, and seemed even taller standing while others sat. Gama's neck warmed, fearing that he'd seen something vanish as well, but the only color on his neck was the soft-green-yellow of relief. She envied his emotion, and shifted back and forth on her feet, anxious for him to speak.

"You want to know how the gathering went in the orchards," Vonti said.

Reln nodded.

"The trees were heavy with fruit," the tall male said. "They're much lighter now. If you're thinking we should abandon this place, I'd say we have enough, we don't need to stay."

Reln pressed his lips together before speaking.

"Thank you, Vonti. You never make me spill more breath than necessary."

Vonti sat again, his head still visible above their brothers' and sisters'. Every throat but Reln's and Vonti's now glowed orange-red with anticipation. Reln was quiet long enough that her sisters and brothers began squirming. The silence went on until Community Hall sent, *Get on with it. Do we stay or go?*

Nervous laughter spread through the room. Reln's face stayed grim.

"We go," he said. "We go now. We'll return later. There's more we need from this place."

The corenta-kin rushed from Community Hall as though fire had erupted inside, making their ways as quickly as possible across the winding paths back to their dwellings to prepare. Gama and Hest hesitated, thinking maybe Reln had more to ask them, but he jutted his chin toward the door in sign that they should go make ready, too.

They hurried out behind the others, running to Home and quickly securing anything lying loose inside—floor pillows, foot casings, bowls and tumblers. Gama had barely finished securing the last window when Reev began quiver and shake, breaking free of the land and rising into the air.

-=o=-

Reev traveled all day, into after-sunend, and settled a short distance from the silver river. At night, with the windows open, Gama heard the water rushing by—coming from an unknown place, going to an unknown place—bringing a sense of calm to the here and now, a sense of things being what they always had been and always would be. She lay awake on her cot, listening to the soft rush of the river, the even pull and push of Hest's breathing, and the nightbirds calling, and tried not to think about all the things that had vanished.

-=o=-

Four bags of brez hair lay poured out onto the floor—the bag Gama and Hest had brought back, and three from other gathering groups. The wood floor had been carefully swept before the bags were emptied, to keep the hair clean. The windows were closed to keep out any breeze, and the air smelled musty and old. Their kin, Palu, Frarm, Kis, and Fel, sat in a circle with them, each with their legs crossed, a big pile of hair coned in the center of the group.

The first step in preparing brez hair to be spun into thread was combing to align the fibers. Gama lifted as big a hank as she could hold and finger-combed it to get the hairs started into the same direction. Several carved-bone combs lay next to her, each with a finer, tighter set of teeth than the next. She picked up the comb with the widest teeth and started combing the hair. In the quiet room, she heard how the comb shushed through the hair.

Usually there'd be chatter among them. Often someone would break into song and they'd all join in. Today everyone was silent, their eyes darting to and from their sisters and brothers or focused hard on their task. A restless energy ran through Gama, and likely through her kin. Combing was tedious, but not hard. It didn't take the kind of concentration the others were giving it.

"Palu," Hest said suddenly, making Palu flinch at his own name. "What song shall we sing? You pick and lead."

Palu stared at Hest a moment, the color on his throat fading to nothing, and said, "I don't feel a song today. Choose someone else, or start it yourself."

Hest shrugged, took in a deep breath, and sang:

> *"Green rises up living from dirt*
> *Into the green come the beast, the bug, and bird*
> *Into green come her sisters, her brothers, and her,*
> *To honor the dirt for its gifts."*

Gama nodded her approval at Hest's choice. It was a companion song. He sang the first verse, they'd all sing the refrain together, and then one of them would sing the next verse, before they all sang the refrain again. Gama liked companion songs—the separateness and togetherness, the celebration of individual and group. It was smart of Hest to choose something in which everyone had a part.

> *"Green is green, rise up new life,"*

Hest began the refrain, but only she joined in.

> *"And sing the sun, the coming light."*

Gama and Hest glanced from face to face. Palu didn't even look up. Fel glanced their way, then back down. Frarm and Kis opened their mouths, but didn't sing. Gama and Hest let their voices trail to nothing.

She set down the hank she was combing and

turned her hands palms up. "I've never known you to pass up a chance to sing, Palu."

Palu shrugged, his head still down, concentrating—or pretending to concentrate—on untangling the long strands stuck in his comb. "Seems foolish to sing when strange things are going on around us."

"Seems foolish not to sing." The wood floor suddenly felt hard and unfriendly. Gama shifted position, trying to get comfortable. "What bothers you more, the disappearing brez or the fact that we broke our routine and landed by the river early?"

Palu let out a noisy breath. "I don't believe the brez disappeared at all. More likely you and Hest scared them away."

Gama opened her mouth to protest, but Palu cut her off. "I'm not saying you told an untruth," he said. "I think the beasts turned and went back into the hills and maybe you two were playing around, the way you do sometimes, and you didn't see them go." He flicked his hand in the air. "Everyone is frightened and worked up over nothing."

Two spots on Fel's neck lit muddy-yellow in indignation. Fel and Hest were close—not as close as Hest and Gama, but close enough that Fel took offense on Hest's behalf.

Gama took offense on her own behalf. "It happened, Palu. We weren't playing around. We were there to work. We took it seriously, as we always do." She locked her eyes on his. "The brez vanished."

Kis touched her throat lightly with one finger. *I*

believe you, he sent to her and Hest, but not the others.

Frarm threw down the comb he'd been using and jumped to his feet. Brez hair flew up in his wake. He pulled the door open but stood inside the jambs, not moving—the brownish-pink of uncertainty glowing on his neck. His hands formed and unformed fists. Gama felt his anxiety like ice on her skin.

"Shut the door, Frarm," Kis said. "A wind comes up, it'll blow the hair all over."

Frarm turned and glared at his corenta-brother. His throat glowed blue-red. "I saw it happen, too." He stepped back and shut the door roughly.

"What?" Hest said, and thought-talked to Gama, *Did he follow us?*

I don't think so, she sent back. *He wasn't at the meadow that I saw.*

The colors on Frarm's throat darkened. He turned to face them and wrapped his arms over his chest, as if suddenly cold.

"I was walking alongside a thin stream that feeds the silver river," he said, his voice quiet, "enjoying the last of the day before sunsetting. A flock of birds flew overhead. Their calls caught my attention. For a moment I watched them flap their wings, heading north. The next moment the sky was empty of anything but a few clouds. I thought it must be a trick of the light. I rubbed my eyes and looked again, the way you do when you're not sure what you saw was real. When I heard about the disappearing brez…" His voice trailed off.

Gama got up and went to the door. She lay her arm over Frarm's shoulders, gently turned him around and walked him back to the others.

"You need to tell Reln," she said. "He needs to know. Everyone needs to know."

Frarm nodded. "But what does it mean?"

FIVE

Voices buzzed inside Community Hall, everyone trying to keep the sound down but the accumulated noise still as loud as standing inside a giant lair of angry insects. More soumyo poured into Hall. The buzz became rushing water, then wild, rock-strewn cataracts. Gama gave up trying to voice-talk to Hest at all. Others had abandoned speech as well, judging by the thought-grains flying around.

Hall's closed doors swung open, banging softly against the walls. Reln strode in and headed straight toward the dais at the rear without a glance or word to anyone. Soumyo began to settle down as he walked by, everyone falling quiet by the time he climbed the steps to the platform. They were silent when he faced the kin and sat near the edge, his legs crossed beneath him—an unusual pose. Speakers stood. It was the way it was done. Reln sitting, Gama noticed, made everyone pay more attention, pull their spines straighter, lean forward.

Reln splayed his fingers on his thighs. "We've all heard what Gama and Hest saw in the meadow yesterday. Disappearing brez! It sounds almost like a hatchling's excuse for not having done their work. But Gama and Hest are no hatchlings and never has either of them been known to slack. Now there's something new to add."

He nodded toward the center of the hall. Frarm slowly pulled to his feet and walked to the dais. Gama knew he'd tell of the disappearing birds. Frarm was as hardworking and trustworthy as she and Hest. The kin wouldn't find comfort in his story.

As Frarm stepped up onto the platform, Reln stood, so that the two were side by side. Frarm told the incident in his usual, plainspoken way. No one broke the silence when he finished, though Gama saw thought-grains passing between some kin. Reln waited long moments for someone to ask a question, voice an opinion, maybe stand and tell something they had seen as well. He waited so long that the quiet began to weigh them down, stifling any words they might have said.

Is there history of these sorts of things happening—maybe log ago? Hest sent to Community Hall, and let Gama hear. *Are we worried for nothing?*

Let me look, Hall sent.

Gama and Hest waited while it searched its long memory for anything that had ever occurred that might be close to beasts and birds disappearing right in front of someone. Hall was nearly as old as Wall. The two of them kept the corenta's history stored in their grains.

No, Hall sent finally. *There've never been happenings like this.*

A tremble ran across Gama's shoulders. Hest sighed quietly.

Reln seemed to have run out of patience with the

long silence. He turned his hands palms up. "If no one has anything to say, best you go back to your dwellings now. Sometimes our minds work better alone than in a crowd. All are welcome to come to my dwelling if there is something private to share."

Everyone came to their feet, some jumping up and heading for the doors quickly, others pushing up slowly, as though through a thick stew—no one speaking. Gama and Hest walked more slowly than normal, no words or thoughts between them. Her stomach felt queasy. She wished that Hall had remembered something. It would be comforting to know others had similar experiences, and to hear how they had gotten through it. Instead, they were alone now in an unknown territory, with no history to guide them.

She heard running feet and turned to see Frarm standing at her shoulder.

"Can I stay with you tonight?" he asked, a little out of breath.

Nerves, she thought. Nerves and fear stealing the air from his lungs.

Frarm glanced at the soumyo around them and dropped his voice low. "Before we came to Community Hall, I told my dwelling-mates what I'd seen. I don't think they believed me. I think they're afraid to believe me, or maybe they suspect something's wrong with me—seeing birds disappear in the sky. Maybe they *want* to believe something's wrong with me." He pulled anxiously at his hipwrap. "You saw what happened to the brez. I know you believe me about the birds. I'd be more comfortable with you two tonight."

Gama could see how comforting it was for others to think that she, Hest, and Frarm had made up their stories or to believe they'd eaten insanity-causing villisity or that stickerbrump had drilled into the soles of their feet—that what they said wasn't real, however much they might believe it. She'd spied it on their necks. It was easier for them to not be around those who had seen strange things with their own eyes—constant reminders that something was going wrong. Gama understood, but she didn't like it.

Home, she sent as they drew near it, *we'll have a guest with us for a while.*

They crossed the last open space between Home and their closest neighbor, but Home didn't open the door like it usually did as they approached.

Why is Frarm with you? it sent.

He's going to stay with us tonight.

Then my door stays shut.

Hest pulled to a stop. *Tell me why.*

Home didn't answer.

Gama put her hand on Hest's arm. She thought she should have touched Frarm instead. He was the one she wanted to distract from wondering why they weren't going inside. "I'm hungry. Can we go to the communiteria before settling in?"

Hest shot her a subtle look—he knew she'd eaten before they went to Community Hall—but he always backed her in anything, same as she would for him.

"I could eat," he said. "How about you, Frarm?"

Frarm shrugged uneasily. "I'm not hungry, but I'll keep you company."

A few other corenta-kin were in the communiteria when they arrived. No one was cooking this late after evening-meal, but cold dishes waited for any who might want them. They'd found a table by the door. Hest sat quietly and devoured a large awa fruit. A bit of juice dribbled onto his chin. Gama reached over and wiped it off, then pushed aside the bowl of vero she'd made herself eat, to keep up her pretense of hunger. Frarm hadn't wanted anything, and stared at nothing in the center of the room. The silence at their table felt louder to Gama than any of the conversations going on around them.

She sent a thought back to Home and let Hest hear it. *Will you say why you don't want Frarm inside?*

Disappearing birds! Home sent. *I don't believe him. He's stirring up disharmony.*

Do you believe Hest and I saw brez disappear?

Even though your blood and sweat isn't in my mortar. I know you would never say what you didn't believe to be true.

Usually a newly emerged member of the corenta would work with her or his dwelling to build it, so that both were happy. But doing that meant tearing down an old dwelling or other structure for materials—destroying that structure's personality. Gama and Hest had chosen instead to move together into Home, which was empty since its occupant had Returned to the creator almost a year before they emerged. Others had done the same before, in other dwellings, with good results. The three of them weren't as close as they'd be if they'd built the dwelling together, but the arrangement had worked well so far.

Frarm believes what he says, too, Gama sent. *You should let him in. Who better than you to protect him at this difficult time? Frarm could have gone anywhere. He chose to ask us—because of you—for shelter. Please don't deny him just one night under your roof.*

Gama didn't know where Home had gotten the inflated sense of self it certainly possessed—likely from its original builder, but sometimes dwellings developed personalities quite different from the soumyo who'd built them. Flattery always worked with Home, and she was not above using silky words when needed.

There was a long silence, then Home sent, *All right. Only for tonight. But you'd all better do a lot of talking. I want to hear the whole story from Frarm. I'll judge the truth of things from that.*

-=o=-

Gama supposed Home felt a little sorry for its attitude, because it listened without interruption to all that Frarm had to say.

I don't know, Home sent when Frarm finished, but it let all three of them hear its thoughts, and that was a good sign. *Things are wrong here.*

In Frarm's story? Something you don't believe?

No, Home sent. *Here. In the world.*

-=o=-

Hest grumbled under his breath. Gama shot a

quick look at his neck. Whatever annoyed him wasn't irritating enough to raise a color on his emotion spots but she knew him well enough to know when his grumbles should be ignored and when he needed to talk.

Gama shifted the wood yoke on her shoulders and jabbed him lightly in the ribs with her elbow. The water buckets on either end of the yoke swung with her movement. "Might as well say it loud enough for everyone to hear."

"This." Hest twisted his body slightly so that the empty buckets on his yoke swung like heavy fruit in a strong wind. His gaze swung across the landscape of stubby brown grass to the river. "If we'd stayed at the meadow, by now it would have rained enough to fill the reservoirs and we wouldn't be out here fetching water by the bucketful."

Frarm and Prill were with them, and Iya and Vonti. Gama was happy Iya had been assigned. She was practical, honest, and not a complainer—three traits Gama appreciated in a workmate. Other units would be making the journey down to the river and back as well. It took a lot of trips to make up for one good rain. But this, with the possible exception of Prill, was the exact crew she would have chosen if it'd been up to her instead of Reln.

"I'd rather be hauling water," Iya said, "than be by a meadow or stream where beasts and birds disappeared into nothing. That meadow made me shiver."

"Not the place itself," Hest said.

Gama finished his sentence, knowing what he

was thinking. "The cause."

"What is the cause?" Iya shifted her yoke on her shoulders. "Either strange things are happening, or my sisters and brothers are imagining things that aren't real. Neither is a good thing."

"It's real," Gama said.

One spot lit blue-red on Frarm's throat and he put up a hand to hide it. Maybe to conceal the color from them, but maybe to pretend to himself that he didn't feel nervous. Gama sent him a supportive smile, but she wished he'd be firmer in his stance. He'd seen what he'd seen with the birds. Better to stand up and face the truth than wish—or pretend—it hadn't happened.

"I don't like it," Iya said. "It needs to stop."

Hest laughed without humor. "I agree."

They reached the stream and one by one set down their yokes on a stretch of sandy bank and unhooked the buckets. The water ran quickly here, and deep below the bank. They lay on their bellies, hanging over the side and reaching the buckets one by one down into the water. Iya grunted at the effort to lift the filled bucket, and long-armed Vonti leaned in to help her pull.

No one spoke while they worked. The quiet made Gama nearly as nervous as thinking about what caused the disappearances—a silence born of fear.

Iya set her last filled bucket on the ground, careful not to spill any water, and said, "Who has a guess at what happened?"

Vonti was on his knees near her, hooking his

four filled buckets onto his yoke. He didn't look up from his work. "I don't mean offense, but honestly I don't think Hest and Gama saw what they think they did. And neither did Frarm."

Gama felt her neck warm. First Palu, and now Vonti. Frarm's dwelling-mates hadn't believed his words either. They'd all known each other since they were hatchlings. Why would anyone think she or Hest or Frarm had suddenly taken up false speaking?

"Why don't you think they saw anything?" Prill said, one spot lighting with hope.

Vonti looked up to answer her. "It's impossible for beasts to vanish from a meadow and birds to disappear from the sky."

"I know what we saw." Gama said, kneeling on the rough riverside sand, hooking her own buckets to her yoke.

"What you think you saw." Vonti leveled the yoke across his shoulders and stood, swinging his shoulders, the yoke moving with them.

A bucket nearly hit her head. Gama jumped up, precious water sloshing from her own buckets. "Might want to be a little more careful, Vonti." She felt a few spots lighting brown-yellow with annoyance. She saw Vonti's gaze settle on her throat and was glad he could see exactly how she felt. "Neither Hest nor I are prone to fancies. You know that. I'm surprised you would insult us with your suggestion."

"Then how do you explain what you saw?" he said. "What happened to the brez?"

"They disappeared. Plain and simple as that. I can't explain how. The ground could have opened up and swallowed them for all we know."

"Like a sinkhole?"

"Maybe." She dropped to her knees again and hooked the third bucket to the yoke. "A sinkhole would explain it. The brez were far enough away that we wouldn't have seen a hole."

Vonti steadied his yoke with one hand and placed the fist of his other hand on his hip. Gama reasoned he was thinking through the possibility.

Prill nodded, her eyes shining. "A sinkhole makes sense." She turned to Hest. "Do you think that's what it was?"

"Only we didn't see them fall," Gama said before Hest could answer "We didn't see them slip into the ground or hear them call out in fear. The sky shimmered and the brez were gone. That's all."

She caught the pinch-mouthed look on Hest's face. *Leave it*, he sent to her. *Let them have an explanation that soothes them. Don't stir things up with truth just for the sake of it. How can we solve this if we are out of harmony?*

Gama didn't know which annoyed her more—Vonti's disbelief or the fact that she understood Hest's point. Her sisters and brothers needed explanations they could believe, reasons to not be afraid. But pretend reasons wouldn't help find the real cause, and they certainly wouldn't give them a way to stop the strange happenings—if they could be stopped. And what if they couldn't? Would all the plants, beasts, and birds of the world disappear one by one? She covered her throat with her hand, to hide the muddy-brown of fear lighting on her spots.

Vonti trained his gaze on Frarm. "What about the birds you saw disappear?"

Frarm drew a deep breath and huffed it out. He looked suddenly exhausted. "Maybe it was the light. Or the birds flew behind some clouds and I just thought they disappeared." He considered for a moment longer, then nodded. "That must be it. Clouds."

Prill's spot changed from the color of hope to the white of satisfaction.

The beasts in the meadow hadn't been hidden by clouds, nor had they fallen into a sinkhole. The brez had been coming towards them one moment and were gone the next. Gama was sure of that. She was sorry now she'd mentioned the sinkhole. She didn't want to be the cause of her sisters and brothers grabbing onto a false security.

Don't let Vonti upset you, Hest sent her. *I know what we saw.*

"What we need," Iya said, hefting her yoke onto her shoulders and standing, "is a song. Hest, you lead us off."

As if a song would make everything all right, Gama thought. She was wise enough not to say it though. In truth, a song was a good idea—a welcome distraction. A way to not think about what crowded everyone's minds. Sometimes a good distraction was just the thing to clear the mind and let new thoughts come in.

Gama lifted her yoke onto her shoulders and stood. "*The Water Song* seems fitting."

Hest nodded, took a few steps, cleared his throat, and sang,

> "*I am the clear water*
> *That glistens in sunlight.*"
> *I fall from the sky*
> *In light and in dark.*"

They all joined in, Vonti, Kis, and Prill singing loudly. Gama couldn't work up the same enthusiasm, even though she thought singing was a good idea. Frarm, she noticed, hardly sang at all. The brez were gone. The birds were gone. No amount of cheerful songs would make that different.

> "*Falling, falling*
> *Kisses on dry land*
> *I am sky's beauty.*"

Hest gulped for breath between verses. Gama knew he'd been singing but thinking, too. Hest never lost breath when he was focused on a song, but if he let his mind wander, he'd need to stop and suck in air. She turned toward him and raised her eyebrow ridges—a clear question. He could think-talk to her if he had something to say. He shrugged and began the second verse as they approached Reev.

> "*I am the dark cloud*
> *That brings the clean water.*
> *I sail the sky*
> *In light and in dark.*"

Hurry! Hurry! Wall sent as they drew close.

They all stopped singing on the same note.

Gama's scalp prickled with sweat. *What's wrong? What's happened?*

I can't say, Wall sent. *It's too horrible. Just hurry.*

They couldn't hurry and risk spilling their precious water, but they sped their steps as much as they dared—their necks all lit with the dark-gray of worry. Gama wanted to throw off the yoke and run.

Wall threw the gate open. *Go to Community Hall*, Wall sent. *Everyone is there.*

Just inside Wall, Gama slipped out from under her yoke, being as fast and careful with the buckets as she could. She ran toward Community Hall, Hest and the others alongside her. Gama hardly saw the structures she rushed past.

Hall opened its doors for them but didn't say anything.

Reln stood on the dais. The soft-green-yellow of relief bloomed on his throat. "We're very glad to see you."

A shiver of nerves ran up her breastbone.

"I don't know any way to say it but plainly," Reln said. "The carding house is gone."

Six

The kin parted, stepping back and squeezing up against the soumyo next to them, to let Gama and Hest through.

"It's one more thing," someone said low as Gama passed by.

"Too many things," said another—words that sounded as though they came from between clenched teeth.

Gama's neck burned and her heart beat hard. The carding house was gone? An entire structure? How could that be?

"Join me at my dwelling," Reln said quietly when they reached him. "We have much to discuss." He looked out across the room and dismissed the assembled kin with a wave of his hand.

Gama watched them go. They were like birds suddenly freed from the pen, she thought—some talking excitedly, some with their heads hung low, as if weighted, colors glowing on their necks—the signs of anxiety, concern, confusion, and shock. She felt her own spots light and change with her shifting emotions while they waited to hear what Reln would say. Hest touched her neck. Gama touched his neck in return—small offers of comfort.

"Shouldn't you go to the communiteria to

answer questions?" Frarm asked, his voice quiet and shaky.

Reln waited until nearly everyone had made their way out the door before stepping down from the dais and answering Frarm. "I'll go as soon as I've spoken with you. We can go together after, if you like."

Gama felt her anxiety like a living thing that had come to dwell within her. She shifted from foot to foot. Reln walked slowly through the nearly empty room without speaking, his hands clasped together behind his back. The six of them followed behind— Hest, Iya, Vonti, Frarm, Prill, and Gama, an edgy procession. If it had been night, the intensity of the colors on their necks would have lit their way. Thought-grains moved through the room. She supposed Reln was think-talking to Hall but had chosen not to let them hear.

Beneath the open sky, Hest sidled up next to Reln and asked the question Gama felt certain pounded through all their thoughts.

"What happened to the carding house?"

Reln gently put his finger to Hest's lips. "Not right here."

Hest's emotion spots flared blue-red with anxiety again, and brownish-pink with uncertainty.

They walked without words—tight, nervous steps—past dwellings, two storage sheds, and a granary. The carding house lay in the other direction—or at least the place where it had stood—empty now, bare dirt, or maybe a hole. Even if she turned, she wouldn't have been able to see anything, not with the way the paths of Reev twisted this way and that. She rubbed her throat to calm herself. She saw Frarm do the same.

The group angled off the main path, taking the thin, winding lane that led to Reln's dwelling. It swung its door open as they approached. Warmth and light flowed out from inside, and the vague scent of aromatics, musky yet sweet. Gama breathed in deeply, longing for the comfort being inside these walls had always brought. Reln's dwelling never spoke much when she was there, but she felt a kindness and a caring from it that some other structures seemed to lack.

Reln gestured for them to sit. His dwelling was large, considering that only he and Prill lived in it. The receiving room was generously sized even for a big dwelling and filled with comfortable, over-stuffed sit-pillows in soft colors that went harmoniously with the pale ocher walls. The six who'd gathered water together glanced at the pillows and one another, but no one sat. Clearly her sisters and brothers couldn't bring themselves to sit and settle any more than she could. Reln remained standing as well.

"Gama. Hest," Reln said. "You know not everyone believed you about the beasts disappearing right before your eyes. Many corenta-kin doubted Frarm's story even more—coming second as it did. No one doubts any of you now, least of all me."

Gama rubbed her hands on her thighs. She should have felt relief, but she didn't. There was little comfort in being believed now only because a structure had disappeared—something everyone could see and no one deny. She didn't want her kin to live with the fear that had shaken her since the first day of the shimmering sky.

"You saw it happen?" she asked.

Reln held his breath a moment, then nodded.

She knew he was relieving the moment, the shock of it—the sense of helplessness. Best to get him talking, she thought. "Was it the same with Carding House—there one moment and gone the next?"

"Mostly," Reln said. "The air shimmered first, and when the structure disappeared there was a creaking sound. Not loud. The kind of sound you think maybe you heard, so you turn your head to look for the source."

"A creak?" Gama said. "Not a hum?"

"I didn't hear a hum."

Gama crossed her arms over her chest, suddenly chilled. "There wasn't a shimmer or a creaking sound when the brez vanished."

"Maybe because Carding House is so big," Hest said. "Whatever took it, maybe there was strain."

"Oh," Frarm said. "I didn't think of that—that something *took* what's gone. I just thought they disappeared. I didn't think of how that could happen."

Gama guessed Iya and Vonti hadn't thought overmuch about the how or what either, since their throats were suddenly aflame with the orange-yellow of confusion and the muddy-brown of fear.

How could they not wonder? Things don't just disappear. *What* took them was the question that had to be answered. And *why*.

"Could it take one of us?" Prill's voice was almost a whisper.

They snapped their gazes toward Reln.

"I don't know," he said, the only answer he could give.

Gama rubbed her thighs. Nothing was certain anymore, but logic said that anything that could make a structure vanish would likely have little trouble with one of them.

"What are we going to do?" she asked, to turn her corenta-kin from worry to devising a plan to avoid losing more of their own.

Reln sank onto a pillow, pulled his knees up to his chest, and sighed. "To protect Reev from something we can't see or even name? I don't know."

From something unknown, Gama thought. She dropped to her knees on a pillow next to him. "Is it just Reev? Are we in the wrong place at the moment these things happen?"

"No," Reln said. "We've been in touch with all the corentas close enough to think-talk with. Most say nothing unusual has happened, but two report that they've had odd occurrences. Kelroosh says all the water in its reservoir dried up in an instant. In Trontin, a female saw a complete orchard disappear. When they sent others to look, the ground was bare, as though no tree had ever stood in that place."

"Like what we saw in the empty field," Hest said, voicing exactly what Gama was thinking. Likely everyone in the room was drawing the same comparison.

"They'd been harvesting that orchard for two generations," Reln said, as though length of time had anything to do with it.

Hest hunkered down on the other side of Reln. "There has to be something we can do."

"We can't stay here," Frarm said. "Maybe it's only in a few territories. We should go near the corentas where nothing has happened."

Reln nodded. "Yes. I've already decided that, and spoken with the other guides. We'll leave this evening and link up with Kelroosh and Trontin in a place where nothing strange has happened. We'll be safe there. You should go now and make ready. If you feel you need to talk more, you're welcome to come to the communiteria with me now."

Hest sent, *Communiteria or back to our dwelling?*

More talk is just more talk, Gama sent. *It won't answer anything. We might as well get ready to move.*

Hest offered a tiny smile, and Gama knew they'd been in harmony of thought as always—he'd only asked from courtesy.

Iya, Vonti, and Frarm must have been think-talking among themselves, because Vonti had no doubt in his voice when he said, "We'll go make ready."

They walked through Reev together until Iya and Vonti broke away to go to their own dwellings. Their paths would take them past where Carding

House had been. Gama didn't envy them the sight and was glad the way to her dwelling led a different direction. Except she wanted to see the place, if only to prove to herself that Carding House was really gone. Funny how that worked—she believed Reln completely, yet still needed to see the proof of his words with her own eyes.

Frarm remained with them until he reached his turn-off.

"Do you want to stay with us again?" Hest asked.

Frarm shook his head. "Everyone knows now that what I said was true. My dwelling and those I share it with want me back. I'd rather be there."

Frarm headed toward his dwelling, leaving Gama and Hest alone on the path. No one else was out. The sound of their feet crunching against Reev's dry soil felt too loud—and lonely.

A thought nagged at her as they made their way toward their dwelling, a thought she didn't share with Hest or Home. If they hadn't known the beasts, birds, and now Carding House would disappear, how could they be sure where it was safe to land?

-=o=-

The bright sun of day-half-gone lit the air when Reev set down in a wild valley full of tall, twisted, red stones—a place not on their usual route. Gama and Hest ran but weren't the first to the gate. All of their kin wanting to see this new place—this fine land where they would be safe—and their new neighbors. Wall was much higher than any soumyo

was tall, but some clever corenta-kin had hiked a
brother or sister onto their shoulders so they could
peek over.

"Can you see them?" those on the ground asked.
"What's out there?"

"Two corentas," a female on her brother's
shoulders said. Her chin rested on the plastered top
of Wall. "One about the same size as Reev, the
other bigger by half."

An excited murmur streaked through the crowd.
"I hope we get to visit," someone said. "I'd like to
see inside another corenta."

Gama rubbed her throat. Had everyone
forgotten what had driven them there? Or had they
resolved not to think about it—to stuff it away and
enjoy these moments. She thought that was more
the case, but Gama felt worry like a deep thrum
under her kin's every excited word and action.

Reln strode up wearing all his marks of
leadership at once—the embroidered shawl of
many colors over his bare shoulders, the black hat
like a bowl turned upside down and with a wide gold
brim, the three thick bracelets on his left arm that
represented their corenta—one bracelet for the
females, one for the males, one for the structures.
He wore a deep-blue hipwrap embroidered all over
with crimson leaves—very different from the plain
beige wrap Gama was used to seeing on him.

"Their gates are opening," someone called from
her perch on a sister's shoulders.

Wall opened its main gate and the soumyo
crowded inside the jambs to look, nudging their

neighbors aside to get a better view. Hest pushed forward, but Gama hesitated. This linking up felt wrong to her. Each corenta had its own course, so that no orchard or meadow was over-plucked, no stream overused for plants or swimmers. Sometimes Gama thought the harmony of their lives depended on everyone conveniently staying out of everyone else's way.

Reln raised his voice to be heard over the excited chatter of the corenta-kin. "The guides are coming. Please make ready to greet them."

Little puffs of dust stirred where those who still rode on a sister's or brother's shoulders jumped down. Gama scrambled with the rest of her kin to form two lines. Guests from another corenta were uncommon, but everyone learned and practiced the traditional ways to greet visitors—ways that likely hadn't changed since the first stones were set to form Wall, Gama thought. The Reev kin knew what to do now without being told.

They're almost here, Wall sent so that everyone heard it. *Have you picked a welcoming song, Reln?*

One emotion spot on Reln's neck lit orange with embarrassment. Gama guessed that with the strain of all that had been happening, their guide had forgotten this gesture of politeness.

"Of course," Reln said aloud. *"The Song of Kinship."*

It was a good choice. Normally they didn't meet with outsiders except at mating sites during Resonance. *The Song of Kinship* declared that no matter what pairing produced the egg or in which corenta the hatchling wound up, it would be considered a full member of that kin. It made sense to sing now of kinship with Kelroosh and Trontin, since they all seemed to need each other, no different than how the members of Reev needed one another. She'd been silly before, to fear this new linking—a natural worry when change seemed quick and inevitable.

Five soumyo came through Reev's main gate, two wearing signs of rank—the guides—and three in plain hipwraps and foot casings. The Reev-kin sang as the outsiders came slowly through the lines formed on either side of the gate, the strangers taking time to look at each Reev-kin and acknowledge them with a flash of nurturing pink. Gama's throat glowed with the dark-red-blue of curiosity.

Gama, Hest, Frarm, Reln sent when the visitors had made it through the lines and the Reev-kin had finished singing, *come with us.*

Hest glanced at her and she shrugged. The three fell in line behind the guides. Reln must have sent the message to all Reev's corenta-kin since no one else tried to follow, though Gama knew her sisters and brothers must have been burning with curiosity.

The guides walked side by side but no one spoke aloud.

Reln swept them all inside his dwelling, gesturing with his chin. They settled onto pillows at his invitation. Gama's stomach felt full of tiny, jumpy beastlets.

Reln nodded toward Trontin's guide, who stood

and introduced himself as Bren and his companion as Joh. Bren was shorter than either Reln or Kelroosh's guide, and stocky. Well-fed. His skin was as red as the day-ending sky and his eyes the color of fertile soil. His voice, when he spoke, had an edge to it, as though sand was grinding in his throat. Joh's skin was so light-red she almost had no color. At Bren's nod, Joh pulled two small boxes from the tools belt at the top of her hipwrap and handed them to her guide.

"Corentas so rarely have the pleasure of meeting other kin along the way," Bren said, his gaze sweeping over everyone in the room. "It's a sorrowful state that has brought our three corentas together, but there still may be joy and new friendships in it. In our travels we pass an area in which the most marvelous stones lie. Please allow me to gift Reev and Kelroosh each with one, in hopes that these troubles will soon pass, we will go our separate ways again, and you will use the stone to be reminded of us, these times and how we triumphed."

He handed one of the small boxes to Reln, and one to Kelroosh's guide. Gama watched, her curiosity rising as they opened the boxes and each drew out a stone about the size of a hatchling's fist. She'd never seen anything like it—crimson, yet so clear she could see Reln's hand through it. Floating inside were flecks of silver, blue, and green. Gama didn't know why, but the stone made her feel happy—and there'd been little of that lately.

Reln nodded toward the other corenta guide, a

female with skin so dark-red it was almost brown, and she rose. She was tall, with long fingers on large hands. She wore an elaborately sewn shawl in every color Gama could imagine—her mark of rank. But her face was kind, and Gama immediately liked her.

She straightened her shawl and said, "I am Kinto." She swept her eyes across two males sitting side by side. "These are my brothers, Cra and Pret."

Cra and Pret looked much alike—same height and weight, same light-red skin, same dark-brown eyes. Gama was glad they didn't wear matching hipwraps, or she wouldn't have been able to tell them apart.

What do you think? she sent to Hest and Frarm, sure that the others were sizing them up the same way they were them—and think-talking to their corenta-kin as well. Thought-grains flew back and forth across the room.

The pinkish one looks nervous, Hest sent.

Joh, from Trontin. She does look nervous. Any guesses why?

Gama saw the obvious truth the moment she sent the question. These were soumyo who'd also seen things disappear. That's why they'd come with their guides—to bring the witnesses together. She sent the thought to Hest and Frarm.

Maybe no one believed her either, Frarm sent.

Everyone believes us now, Hest sent.

Gama thought of the carding house and worried again for it. Had it been frightened? Was it frightened still, wherever it was? What could snatch up an entire structure with no more effort than she lifted a bucket of water?

Kinto held her stone in her outstretched palm. "We are touched, Bren, by your gift. The soumyo of Kelroosh will treasure it always." She closed her long fingers around the stone and let her arms fall in front of her. "As Bren said, it is a sorrowful state that has brought us here together. There may be safety in this place, but safety is not guaranteed. We must find the source of the danger. We can't defend against what we don't know."

Gama's gaze flitted between the two leaders. Bren had fine manners, but Kinto of Kelroosh seemed more likely to get things done. If Reln partnered with Kinto, Gama was sure the two of them could find a way past the fear festering in the corenta-kin now.

"Hest and Gama," Reln said, startling her from her thoughts. "I've told the guides about the carding house, which I witnessed, and a bit about what you saw. I'd like you to tell it in your own words."

They told the story again, the words no easier to say the second time than they'd been the first. Their guests listened with little expression on their faces but their emotions spots showed the purple-gray of concern and the blue-red of anxiety.

"You were together?" Bren from Trontin asked.

Gama nodded. "But Frarm was alone."

All eyes shifted to him. He told about the birds, his voice suddenly strong and confident. He didn't hint that perhaps the birds had vanished into the clouds the way he had with Vonti. He knew what he'd seen as clearly as she and Hest did.

Kinto, the Kelroosh guide, said, "Cra and Pret have a similar tale."

Cra's neck glowed blue-red and he stared at his hands as if they were something new and unknown to him. Gama thought his anxiety came as much from shyness as anything. Pret did the talking.

"Cra and I were up early one morning," Pret said, "before chore hour, and we decided to go to a nearby river and see if we could catch a grenlo or two. The reeds are thick by this river—or had been thick, the day before when we visited. When we arrived, not one reed thrust from the water. Nothing swam in the waters or crawled along the banks. It was as if someone had come along and taken everything live that was there, put it in a bag and carried it away."

Gama's head hurt, remembering the grain fields, and trying to imagine what could pluck up every reed, every beast that swam or crawled. Trying to think of why someone or something would do that.

Bren from Trontin lay his hand on Joh's neck. Joh's spots burst into color—orange-red of anticipation, blue-red of anxiety.

"Please tell your story," Bren said.

The pinkish female covered her throat with her hand, but let it drop when she started talking. The color on her neck was as bright as before, and Gama wasn't surprised that her voice quavered when she spoke.

"I was with my brothers in our dwelling. It was after night-meal. We were talking and playing a game—the three of us. Suddenly the air in the room took on a kind of shimmering, like pond water that's been lightly disturbed by wind. Then my brother was gone. Vanished right in front of my eyes."

Gama's chest felt like a band had tightened around it. This answered Prill's question—the soumyo were no safer than the beasts or birds.

Joh's neck erupted in a new color—the pale-blue of despair. Bren stroked her neck, but she pushed Bren's hand away and locked eyes with Gama. "My brother was gone. Is gone. Where did he go?"

Gama wished she had an answer for her.

Reln sighed and pulled himself up off his pillow. "We'll be in contact," he told the Kelroosh and Trontin guides. "Tell you anything we learn as soon as we learn it."

Kinto and Bren rose and moved to the door, their kin following.

When they walked out, all the kin of Reev stood waiting outside the door. Gama judged by their anxious expressions that Reln's dwelling had told the kin and structures everything said inside it. Wall likely had told the other corentas.

One of the males, Grik, stepped in front of Reln. "What are you going to do about it?" he asked. Demanded, more like. Subtlety and patience were never strong in him, but it was the question in every mind, and it needed an answer.

"We are all confused and frightened." Reln's eyes were on Grik but his voice loud enough for everyone to hear. "Our thoughts chase each other in useless circles and we may find ourselves caught in that fear. We may want to place blame. We must focus instead on solutions. Reach out to your corenta-kin with think-talking, so we remember that we are all one. Speak with the structures. Test your ideas. Build one thought upon another until the solution is found. For now, we are safe in this place. We have food enough to last us a while. We have time to think and plan."

He swept his gaze across the soumyo standing before him. "All work will be suspended. Go to the communiteria and the storage houses and gather what you will need for a five-day wait. Any news from the other corentas will be shared among us all as soon as anything is known."

A female standing next to Gama opened her mouth to speak. Reln silenced her with a look and strode through the crowd toward the communiteria. The soumyo parted for him, but stayed rooted where they stood.

"Come on," she said to Hest. "Someone has to be first."

They sidled their way through the crowd after Reln. Their sisters and brothers fell in behind.

-=o=-

Gama bolted awake to Home softly crooning *Kroot kroot* to get her attention. The night was deep and dark. Home had never woken her at night before.

Frarm was with them again. He felt more comfortable with kin who'd also seen something strange and knew the truth of it in their hearts, he'd said. Gama had guessed that his dwelling-mates still loved him, but didn't particularly want him around, as though seeing strange things might be catching. In the thin light, she could make out Frarm- and Hest-shaped lumps on their cots. Both slept fitfully, turning first to one side and then to the other, as though they couldn't find a way to be comfortable.

What is it? she sent to Home.

Something is here, Home sent.

What do you mean—something?

I can't say. There are no words, no pictures I can send you. But something is here. I feel it.

Her breath was shallow in her chest. Home was right. Something felt wrong with the room, with the air. Wrong in the same way that the shimmer in the sky was wrong. She couldn't put words to it either, couldn't describe what made her skin feel suddenly clammy, or the air seem cold and thick.

Hest rolled over and sat up, a movement of shadow in the room. *I feel it too.*

The air grew thicker, colder, harder to breathe. Hest coughed, and Gama made out the quick movement of his hand covering his mouth, trying to stifle a second. It didn't matter, though. Whatever was there saw them, or smelled them, or had some other way to track them. It knew every move they made—Gama felt that as true.

Frarm pulled his blanket tight around himself—a small movement that Gama could barely see in dim room *Why is it so cold?* Frarm sent. *I'm shivering.*

Both of you, she sent, *come to my cot. I think we should be close, keep hold of each other.*

72

Hest threw off his covers but walked slowly, as if afraid to bump into something in the empty space between his cot and hers. When he reached her, he sat gingerly and took her hand. She squeezed back and made sure they both had a firm hold.

You come too, Frarm.

He slung his legs over the side of his cot, but froze there.

The air began vibrating, the individual bits bouncing against her skin. As cold as the room had felt before, it turned warm now. Sweat beaded on her scalp. She squeezed Hest's hand tight.

Come be with us, she sent to Frarm. *Quickly. It's safer if we're together.*

Was that true? Anything that could snatch up Carding House could likely grab three little soumyo as easily as she could pick up a gathering basket. But it would feel safer if they were together.

Frarm seemed to gather his courage and jumped from his cot—the thud of his feet hitting the floor sounding as loud as thunder to her. He didn't walk slowly as Hest had. He ran, leaning so far forward that halfway across the room he stumbled and nearly fell. He pulled himself upright and stopped. Gama locked her eyes on his, as though her gaze could drag him the rest of the way.

A strange noise joined the pressing air in the room—like whirling bugs skimming past her earholes. And behind that, a low hum. And a faint smell, like something bitter burning a distance away. Hest coughed again. Her gaze slid to him for a bare moment.

When she looked back, Frarm was gone.

"Hest!" she yelped, and thought-talked, *Frarm, where are you? Are you all right? Frarm!* No reply came back. Worry blasted through her. Her spots flared blue-red. One spot lit soft-green-yellow—relief that it hadn't been Hest who was taken. Or her.

Home called to the other structures, likely telling the other structures what had happened. Her chest felt tight, her muscles cramped. The heavy chill in the air lifted and she managed to send Home a request to turn up the lights. Frarm's cot was empty of anything but his crumpled blankets. Her heart pounded against the cage of her ribs.

"What happened?" she whispered to Hest.

"I don't know," he whispered back. He put his arm around her shoulders and pulled her close.

Are we next?

"I don't know," he said.

Get out! Home sent. *Get out now!*

They ran. Home threw open its door. Reln stood just outside the door and grabbed her hand as she crossed the threshold. It looked like all their sisters and brothers had fled their dwellings too. Why not? Staying indoors hadn't protected Frarm.

"Go to Community Hall." Reln's voice was low and firm. "Calm yourselves. We'll need you to tell us what happened."

Her mouth felt dry and her neck hot from the colors flaring on her emotion spots. Hest wasn't doing any better. He tried to send her a thought but it was jumbled. They followed Reln's orders and went straight to Community Hall, only half-seeing their corenta-kin standing with Reln and staring after them.

Hall had opened its door only a little way. Gama had to turn sideways to slip through. The structures had been talking to each other in their own speech as she and Hest made their way across Reev, but Hall turned silent the moment she passed its jambs.

They walked all the way to the front of Hall—the further they were from their dwelling the better Gama felt—but didn't step up to the dais. They hunkered down on the floor pillows instead, close to each other, shoulders and hips touching. Gama hoped Reln wouldn't make them stand up there with him. She knew it was a false hope. Their sisters and brothers would want the whole story and she and Hest were the only ones left who could tell it.

"You tell it," she whispered to Hest. She couldn't bear the thought of describing the moment of Frarm's disappearance, of losing a brother—it was too awful.

"You woke up first," he whispered back. "You saw more."

"Felt it before I saw anything." A tremble ran across her shoulders as she remembered the odd way the air felt. The sensation that something unknown was there among them.

"You'll have to tell it," Hest said. "I'll pick up the story as soon as I can."

She rubbed her thighs with both hands and nodded.

Hall's wide double-doors flung open and banged against the walls. Their corenta-kin flooded inside, their necks ablaze, cutting off conversations as they crossed the threshold. Her heart beat double-time, watching them find pillows and sit, watching Reln walking fast toward her and Hest.

"Come." Reln clearly expected them to follow him onto the dais.

Gama and Hest climbed up. Reln gave her a look. She drew a deep breath and began.

Her sisters and brothers listened in the silence manners demanded, but she saw their throats flash with the color of their emotions—gray-red with shock, red-blue with anxiety, brownish-pink with uncertainty. Here and there a throat lit with the soft-green-yellow of relief—glad in their hearts that it was Frarm and not them. She almost stopped talking, seeing that, and felt her own throat warm with the gray-green of revulsion. Yet she'd felt the same relief that it hadn't been Hest or her.

When she reached the part of the story where Hest woke, he stepped forward and took it from there.

"We couldn't see much in the darkness," he said, "but each of us, especially Home, felt something was wrong."

Listening to Hest brought the memories back more clearly than telling them had. Her stomach fluttered and her throat lit purple-gray with worry for Frarm, worry about her brothers, sisters, and corenta--what these events meant and what might happen in the future. She glanced at Reln and saw the same color on his throat.

She heard Hall talking to the other structures in

their own language, likely sharing Hest's words with them. It was easy to see how their corenta-kin felt, but impossible with the structures. A soumyo couldn't know what a structure thought or felt unless it chose to say. Were most of the structures as panicked as Home had been, or as calm as Hall seemed to be? Better to wonder about that than think on what had taken Frarm.

Hest finished talking and stepped back.

"What do we do now?" someone in the back yelled. "Nowhere is safe. No one is safe."

Hall's doors swung open and Vonti ran into the hall. Gama, Hest, and Reln saw him first, from their places on the dais. His neck was lit gray-red with shock and dark-gray with worry. Gama felt her own neck warm, her colors a match for Vonti's. She held her hand out toward him. All the seated kin turned to follow Gama's gaze.

Vonti blinked quickly a few times. "The food is gone." His voice was raspy with despair. "Reln sent me to check on it when Gama's dwelling sounded the alarm. I've searched the communiteria, the storage houses, all the dwellings. There're scraps, but most of the food has vanished."

Voices rose up, wild bursts of sound that Gama couldn't make sense of. A question would float loud above the general noise, then sink in the rising tide of words. Reln raised his arms for quiet, but the corenta-kin were caught in their own concerns, their own fears. From the dais, Gama watched some of her sisters and brothers storm out the doors. She saw corenta-kin clutching each other, and wide-eyed Vonti surrounded, his brothers and sisters throwing questions at him. His neck flashed blue-red with anxiety, then orange-yellow with confusion. She jumped from the dais and cut through the crowd, shouldering aside those who pressed at him. She elbowed her way to stand next to him and leaned in to speak in his earhole.

"Do you have any more to say, Vonti? Anything to add?"

He shook his head. His emotion spots changed colors so quickly, it was hard to keep track of his feelings.

"Do you want to stay here?"

He shook his head again.

She grabbed his arm and pulled him to the door. Hest came up beside them and stepped in front, gently nudging aside anyone who tried to ask Vonti more questions or block their way.

The corenta-kin who'd gone outside were rushing toward their dwellings. Gama didn't know what they expected to find—that Vonti had told an untruth? That the food was still there? She didn't know which frightened her more—Frarm's disappearance, their food being gone, or corenta-kin beginning to doubt each other's words.

Vonti's dwelling opened the door only a crack when they reached it, little different than how Hall had greeted Hest and her. Vonti ran his hands over his face and sighed loudly.

"Thank you, Gama. Everyone kept asking the same questions—was the food really gone? Was I sure? Had I checked their dwelling?" He threw up his hands. "What could I tell them? Yes, I kept saying, yes, but they wouldn't stop. They kept asking."

Hest stroked his throat, to comfort him. The colors on Vonti's throat slowly paled.

"I'm going inside," Vonti said. "Thank you."

They nodded and turned. Gama heard the soft thunk of the door shutting firmly behind them.

They didn't talk on the path back to their dwelling. What words were there to say? Gama wasn't surprised when Home didn't throw open the door as they approached. It was frightened too. Carding House had disappeared, which meant structures were at risk just like birds, beasts, and soumyo.

We're here, she sent, even though they were certainly close enough for Home to sense them. The door still didn't open.

Is something wrong?

Home sent, *Go away. Go away, the both of you.*

Please, Home. Open your door.

No, it sent. *You saw the beasts, and the beasts disappeared. You worked in Carding House, and it vanished. Frarm came to stay, and Frarm is gone. You've drawn this misery inside our walls. I won't let you in.*

SEVEN

They stood outside Home, stunned.

Turn around and walk away no different than we would on any other day, Gama sent to Hest, too angry to speak out loud and let Home hear the panic she felt.

We should talk to Home, he sent back. *Reason with it. You've convinced it to change its mind before.*

Panic and anger bubbled in her—showing on her throat. She knew Home, its stubborn streak. It was unlikely to change its mind. She turned her back toward their dwelling. *Home won't let us in. Maybe later, but not now. We need tell Reln what's happened, and find a place to stay until Home comes to its senses.*

Hest touched one of the spots glowing like fire on her throat. *All right. Let's find Reln.*

Gama put her hand over the back of her neck and walked with her head down. Panic that could be seen could easily be spread. She lifted her head once they'd gotten nearly halfway to Reln's and she'd begun to feel calmer.

Prill met them at the door. Gama's spots had quieted, but still showed enough color that one blue-red spot of anxiety bloomed on Prill's own throat in response.

"Reln," Hest said, and Gama looked past Prill at their guide coming toward the door.

The words tumbled out of her. "Home won't let us inside. It blames us for the strange things that have happened. The brez disappearing, and the empty fields. And for Frarm. But Hest and I didn't do anything. It was just circumstance. We have nowhere to stay."

Reln reached out to touch her throat, then seemed to think better of it.

"You can stay here until this is straightened out," he said. "I'll go tomorrow and speak with your dwelling myself."

-=o=-

Alone, Gama paced in the sleeping quarters Prill, Hest, and she now shared, restless, her mind churning. Hest and Prill had woken early, but Gama knew Hest was waiting for her to join him in the receiving room. She felt odd and alone without Hest, but she didn't feel like rushing to meet him either. Prill's hipwraps, cloaks, and foot casings lay strewn everywhere. Gama kicked a hipwrap, watching the fabric lift into the air and fall back to the floor.

At least Prill didn't seem to mind sharing with Hest and her. Was glad for the company, Gama thought. Three nights had passed since Home had turned them away, and their dwelling still wouldn't have them back, no matter what Reln said—a breach of manners nearly as strange as any of the other recent occurrences.

May I ask a question? Gama sent to Reln's dwelling as she secured Prill's fallen cloak on a wall peg.

81

Of course, the dwelling sent. *But note before you do that I am known for truthfulness, not kindness.*

Gama nodded, though she was never sure how much physical movement structures could read. In any event, she preferred truth to false kindness.

Are you frightened by Hest and me? Uncomfortable having us here?

No, the dwelling said. *I don't believe you have brought these troubles to us, though others do.*

She rubbed her hands on her thighs. *Is Prill frightened of us?*

You must ask Prill that question.

Gama nodded again and exhaled. She'd talk to Prill, find out how she felt. And to Reln. As guide, he didn't have much choice but to take them in. It could be that Prill and Reln would be happier if they stayed elsewhere—if there was an elsewhere that would take them.

She pulled on her cloak. Hest was waiting in the receiving room. No matter what nerve-rattling things were going on around them, work and chores still had to be done.

She was assigned to the spinners that day with Vonti and Iya. Hest was assigned to the granary. It wasn't unheard of for her and Hest to be assigned separately, but it wasn't usual either. Reln had his reasons for separating them, she was sure, though she couldn't guess what they might be.

-=o=-

The brez hair they'd carded had been moved before the carding house disappeared. Now it waited to be spun into thread for the weavers.

They'd each done this before, enough times that the spinners had left the room open and the spindles and brez hair waiting for her, Iya, and Vonti. Vonti hadn't looked at or spoken to her since she'd arrived—not the way it usually was, those assigned the work for the day laughing if someone pulled the roving too hard and broke it, or mocking the full-time spinners behind their backs for their frustrations with the learners.

There'd be plenty to irritate the spinners today. Gama's hands felt slick with nervous sweat. Vonti had his spindle between his knees, but couldn't get an even rhythm going.

"We're all a little nervous today," Iya said, her hands slipping off her own spindle.

Vonti looked at Iya and then Gama, his face carefully bland. He turned his attention back to the spindle. Iya raised her eyebrow ridges and hiked one shoulder in a shrug. Gama watched them both a moment, then gave Vonti a gentle jab in the side with her elbow. "Nothing to say?"

He kept his eyes on his work.

She was fairly certain what he was thinking. Thoughts unspoken had a way of festering. Her voice dropped low. "Afraid you might disappear like Frarm if you're with me?"

"No." Vonti's long fingers pricked at the roving around his wrist, trying to loosen it. "It is strange though that you seem to be there so often when things happen."

"And Hest," she said. "Are you blaming us?"

"Your dwelling does."

"Do you?"

The spindle between Vonti's knees slipped and fell over. He picked it up and threw it across the room. "I don't know what I think." He pulled himself to his feet and stomped out of the room.

Iya sniffed and rubbed her nose.

Gama stared at the door Vonti had slammed behind him. "He shouldn't have left. We should have talked it out. Reln was right—if we don't stick together, fear will destroy us."

-=o=-

Prill pushed the chest that held her personal goods toward the center of the room. She could have simply asked the dwelling to draw the metal screens over the sky-window each night—or chances were the dwelling, knowing her preference for dark, would have done it itself—but Prill liked the physical act, she'd said—climbing onto the chest, the way the screen felt in her hands, the sounds of the chest sliding across the wood floor and the moving screen made.

Gama watched her, a bubble of anxiety forming behind her breastbone. "Prill. Leave it tonight. Please."

Prill stopped pushing the chest and looked up.

Gama felt her neck warm. "It's silly, but tonight, I'd like the moon and starlight. The dark—"

"Of course," Prill said, and began dragging the chest back into the corner.

-=o=-

Prill's breathing was deep and even—fast asleep. Star and moonlight dimly lit the sleeping quarters. It wasn't much light, but Gama was glad for it. She could barely make out the shape that was Hest, but knew he was awake by the soft creak of his cot as he turned restlessly.

Kis' dwelling turned him out today, she sent to him.

Why are you still awake? he sent back.

Same reason you are.

The structures, he sent. *We have few friends among them these days.*

Community Hall took Kis in. It hasn't turned against us, but I sense Wall getting prickly. She rolled her shoulders, wondering if she should say what bothered her—the worrisome thought scratching at the back of her mind, then sent, *What if Reev decides it's better off without us? You and me. Some of the others.*

Hest's cot creaked. In the thin light, Gama saw he was in his thinking position—his body still, his eyes wide, staring at nothing. He didn't answer.

She drew a breath and let it out. *Reev can't decide that though, can it? It would be like deciding you didn't want a part of yourself any more. Even with some of the structures acting strangely, it's not like all of Reev is siding with a few scared dwellings. I'm certain Home and Kis' dwelling will come to their senses. Probably be embarrassed about how they acted. Reev wouldn't suddenly decide it didn't want us any more than the corenta-kin would suddenly abandon the structures and live outside its walls. It's as unthinkable as you and me splitting apart.*

Gama waited, but Hest didn't respond. Still thinking, she supposed, and not ready to share. Hest could be secretive that way. She was used to it, but that didn't stop his silence from being annoying—and hurtful.

An odd thought jumped into her head, a thought like words sounding in her mind—Hest was being difficult for no reason. The males were different, with their one soft little hand and one hard digger claw. They had brought the troubles to Reev. They were cagey and plotted to get things their own way, not thinking of the good of the whole. Wasn't that what Hest was doing now? Lying there so quietly, thinking about himself? Vonti had stomped off, leaving her and Iya to finish his work. The males should be driven out.

But that was wrong. Home had refused her entrance just as it had Hest. Except, when she thought about it, everyone else who'd been turned away was male. Maybe it was just Hest Home didn't want inside. Maybe she could go back and live there.

She sent Home the question—her thought-grains moving through the darkened room like tiny dull lights.

Yes, it sent back. *You may return. It's Hest who is no longer welcome.*

Gama pulled the coverlet tight over her chest, as if that would slow her suddenly speeding heartbeats. She could go back, stay again where she was happiest, most comfortable.

But without Hest.

Why not Hest? she sent.

Have you not noticed? Home sent back. *When bad things happen, a male is always there. No bad thing has happened with only females around. Males bring the bad things to us. I cannot be safe with a male within my walls.*

Gama sucked air across her teeth. Home had been thinking along the same lines she had.

I was there, too, Gama cautiously sent. She didn't want Home to change its mind about letting her in. *I was there when the beasts disappeared, and when Frarm vanished.*

She thought again that probably she and Hest should have built their own dwelling rather than moving into an existing one. A dwelling they'd built together, with their blood and sweat mixed into its mortar, would never have turned either of them away. Kis had made the same mistake they had—moving into an already built structure.

Will you be coming back? Home sent.

She felt her neck warm with the bright-greenish-blue of wanting. To sleep in her own cot. To have her own things around her, placed where she wanted them. To not feel forced to walk stealthily, trying to stay out of Reln's and Prill's way.

Without Hest.

Without. Hest.

She ran her hand over her scalp. *I'll stay here a while longer.*

Home breathed a long, windy sigh. *Best be careful then. Two males under one roof with you and Prill—anything could happen. And tell Reln, the soumyo need to make things right for all of Reev. It's his responsibility. He must do something quickly.*

-=o=-

"What do the structures expect us to do?" Reln swirled the drink in the tumbler he held. The communiteria was nearly full but strangely quiet. Reln kept his voice down. "They must know that if there was some way to stop this upheaval, we would."

Gama rubbed her hands on her thighs. "I told Home I'd tell you what it said, and I have."

Reln shook his head. "Your dwelling isn't the only one. Community Hall, Wall, my dwelling, others—they're all demanding we stop whatever is happening from happening anymore."

"How are the soumyo supposed to do that?" Hest said.

She knew Communiteria was listening to their conversation and would spread it to all the structures of Reev. Once the structures knew, the corenta-kin would know as well. Reln needed to offer some kind of plan—something to help them all feel safe.

Prill looked down at her hands, resting on the table. "Yesterday five of our sisters stopped me on my way back from the storage sheds. They wanted to know how full or empty they were. I told them nearly empty."

Reln nodded. "That's true. We're going to have to send a foraging group out soon."

The blue-red of anxiety was bright on Prill's neck. She didn't look up. "They said our troubles were the males' fault. That male energy brought these difficulties to us."

Hest's eyes widened, but he kept silent. Reln

didn't say anything either.

"How could that be possible?" Even as Gama spoke, she remembered thinking the same way in the night, remembered their dwelling saying it wouldn't let Hest back in. Maybe these sisters knew something. She shifted her gaze to Hest. He was staring hard at Prill.

Prill kept her eyes focused on the tabletop.

"Maybe you should send an all-female foraging group out." Gama thought for a moment. "I'll go. I'll take the lead, if you want—or follow whomever you choose."

Reln looked happy at the suggestion—or the gesture of support, she didn't know which—but said, "It won't make any difference. All female, all male, or mixed, the danger is the same." He set his tumbler down. "I'm Reev's guide. I'll go, but I will take only males with me."

She felt Hest staring at the back of her neck.

I have to tell you something, he sent. *Last night I had the strangest thought—so strong, I heard it in my mind like spoken words. I thought that the females had brought this grief to our lives. That we males would be safe if we could get the females to leave Reev. But then I thought, if the females left, you would leave, too. I wouldn't want that.*

A cold shiver ran through her. She glanced up and took in the room. Almost all the soumyo of Reev were here, as they were every day for morning meal, but now males mostly sat with males, females with females. Their table was one of the few that was mixed.

-=o=-

Five sisters were in the receiving area when Gama walked out in the morning. Everyone turned their heads to look as she entered the room—the five, plus Reln, Prill, and Hest, all sitting stiffly on the floor pillows. On a few necks, Prill's among them, the red-pink of certainty lit, as if they already knew where Gama stood. She didn't know what had brought them to this room.

Hest sent, *You might want to stay out of this. Spare yourself some* grief.

Seems to be too late for that, she sent back.

Reln gestured toward an empty pillow lying between him and Prill. "Join us, Gama. I'd like to hear your opinion. These sisters," he spread his hands to acknowledge the visitors, "have some thoughts on the cause of the strange happenings."

Gama settled onto the large red pillow between Reln and Prill and glanced among the visiting females, trying to guess who would take the lead.

Reln nodded to Mahn. Gama wasn't surprised. Mahn—a stocky, reddish-brown female with watery yellow eyes—had a need to be seen as involved in everything.

Mahn didn't speak immediately. She held off, forcing everyone in the room to give her their full attention.

"Tethyod," she said, and let the word hang in the air.

Reln's lips tightened, but if he was offended or appalled, he gave no other sign. Hest showed nothing on his neck or face either. Gama listened for thought-talk, but evidently Hest had nothing he wanted to say to her.

Tethyod was the word for male energy, the counterbalance to yononsa—female energy. Gama's neck warmed at the implication.

"How do you reason that?"

Mahn drew herself up tall. "Males have been present at each occurrence. I've spent a good deal of time thinking and feeling on the question. I've seen the truth of it: the males *brought* the occurrences."

Gama remembered the odd thought she'd had in the night, the same thought Mahn was putting forth now—that the males *were* at fault here. And Hest had thought it was the females who'd brought these troubles to Reev. A small chill ran across her shoulders.

"I was there a few times, too," she said. "Why not blame the females equally? Why is any of this anyone's fault? It could be something natural. You might as well blame the males for snow that falls unexpectedly during First Warmth."

Mahn's sister Du leaned forward. "Do you think this is a natural occurrence, Gama?"

Gama drew in a breath. Mahn was the voice but Du the brain of these two. It was clear who'd concocted this theory.

"Not natural, no," she said. "But not the fault of anyone we know either."

Mahn smiled thinly. "Not intentionally. I didn't say the males had brought these troubles on purpose. But there is something in their tethyod, in their maleness and essential makeup, that is drawing the troubles to Reev—and to Trontin and Kelroosh."

Reln and Hest sat still and quiet.

Why aren't you speaking up, Hest?

Gama, he sent, and then sent nothing more.

Tell me what you're thinking, she sent.

I think she is part right. Maybe males and females living together makes no more sense than two corentas joining together. The more I think about it, the more I see there's something wrong about it.

She felt her mouth drop open and two spots flare dark-yellow-green in surprise. The others would have seen that—seen the thought-grains moving. They might guess Hest and she were think-talking, or they might decide her surprise came from realizing Mahn and Du were right. Gama cared only about Hest.

That makes no sense. We've always lived together. These new things that are happening—they come from the outside.

Hest ran his soft hand over his scalp. *I knew you wouldn't see.*

She'd been so focused on him, she'd not been listening to what Du was saying.

"There are many of us, Reln." Du leaned toward him "We are in harmony on this point. Females and males must separate, each with their own inside Reev."

Brown-purple burst into light on Reln's throat. Exasperation. "You are not guide here, Du. It's not your decision to make."

"Not yet," Mahn muttered.

Gama swung her gaze to her. Her stomach

clenched. Too much was happening at once—the disappearances, her odd thoughts in the night, Hest's opposite echo of her own thoughts, and now, Mahn and Du. "I won't listen to this." Her words came out sounding harsher than she would have wanted, but being polite was the least of her worries. She stood and strode out the door.

Reln's dwelling didn't shut the door immediately behind her. Maybe Reln expected her to come back inside and apologize. He'd wait a long time for that.

"Gama," Hest called, running after her. "Gama!"

She kept going a few paces, then turned and faced him. His throat was awash with the sorrow-color. Sorrow that he agreed with Du and Mahn? That angered her more.

"We've never been out of harmony like this, Hest. What is going on?"

He ran his smaller hand over his scalp. "Realization. Seeing clearly that things are changing."

Anger, confusion, and her own sorrow stilled her tongue. She glanced around Reev, seeing her sisters and brothers going about their business as always. And the difference—males with males, females with females.

"Home invited me back," Hest said. "I'm going."

Her anger dropped a notch and she smiled. "I'm glad Home came to its senses. I'd rather be there than with Reln and Prill."

He stared at the ground. "Only me. I'm sorry, Home says you're not welcome. I'm sorry."

Her neck exploded into color—gray-red with shock and orange-yellow in confusion. Home had told her it was Hest it didn't want within its walls.

"Why?" she managed after a moment.

"You missed some of Reln's meeting with Mahn and Du." Hest cleared his throat. "They've united many—most—of the females behind them. They call themselves Doumanas—females who don't wish to live with males. Home felt—you know how Home is, contrary for the sake of it sometimes— that if the females were going to band together, it preferred males. This male at least. Me."

Her mind spun. "This is madness, Hest. Females and males built Reev and every other corenta together. We are soumyo—male and female making up one whole. You can't throw half of yourself away."

When Home had invited her back, she hadn't gone. She'd chosen to stay with Hest. Why did he find it so easy to abandon her now?

Hest looked out across the commons.

"I'm moving back with Home," he said. "It'd be a good idea for you not to stay with Reln any longer. Find a sister willing to share her dwelling. Live there."

She grabbed his hand. "Hest."

"Don't Gama. I hate leaving you. I hate that it's not your fault, or my fault, but it has to be. The separation is the only thing that makes sense." He pulled his hand free and walked away.

"How does it make sense, Hest?" she called, running after him. "Explain it to me."

He turned. "It's obvious, isn't it? Since we've started talking about keeping male and female apart, nothing has disappeared."

She stared after him as he turned again and walked off, the spots on her neck so hot they were like fire on her skin.

-=o=-

Gama caught sight of thought-grains floating into the room.

Please join us in the receiving area, Reln sent.

A tingle ran up her spine. Lately every conversation with Reln centered on something that had gone wrong. She hurried down the hallway, but wished it was a longer trek.

Six or seven corenta-kin sat on floor pillows or stood in the receiving room, along with Prill and Reln. Hest wasn't there, which disappointed her, but neither were Du or Mahn—and she was glad for that.

"We're almost out of what food we scavenged earlier," Reln said, wasting no time getting to the point. "We have to leave Reev today and look for more outside our wall."

She heard a few quick intakes of breath and someone cleared his throat nervously, but no one spoke. Gama looked again at the others in the room, more carefully this time. Reln had chosen well, she thought. With the exception of Prill, these soumyo were probably the boldest and quickest thinking among the corenta-kin—exactly who she'd want with her in dangerous times, though she'd have added Hest to the group. His absence felt like a gap that no one else could fill.

Reln glanced at Prill, and for a moment Gama hoped he'd say Prill wouldn't be coming with them. It would be a lie to say that even the bold weren't going to be worried and afraid outside the wall. They were worried and afraid inside the wall. Having the nervous, hesitant Prill with them wouldn't make anyone feel braver.

Prill rose and went into the dwelling's small communiteria. She returned with a long rope.

Reln tucked it between his elbow and side while he put on his cloak. "I can't guarantee this will protect us, but if we're lashed together, we'll either all be safe or mutually disappeared."

There was some laughter at that—the nervous kind. Reln didn't smile.

It made sense to her. She and Hest had been holding tight to each other when Frarm disappeared. Maybe the whatever-it-was could only take one soumyo at a time, though it didn't seem to have any problem taking a whole herd of brez.

Gama ran back to the sleeping quarters to pull on her foot casings. By the time she returned to the receiving room, the others had left, leaving the door open for her to follow. They were a short distance ahead. She hurried to catch up.

Few other soumyo were out as they made their way toward Wall and the north gate. Those who did see them watched with solemn eyes as they passed.

-=o=-

They stopped just inside the gate and lashed themselves to their neighbors, with plenty of loose rope between so they wouldn't be hindered at their work. A male who wasn't going with them handed out gathering bags. His neck was blue-red with anxiety. Gama's own spots lit in sympathy to his worry. She rubbed her throat hard. Adding someone else's worry to her own was the last thing she needed.

Reln must have coordinated with the guides from Kelroosh and Trontin. Small groups, lashed together the same as they were and carrying their own baskets and tools, came out of their gates and joined them—Trontin's first, and further along, Kelroosh's.

There was no singing, no words at all, no thought-grains moving between close kin, as though each one of them was alone. They walked in a silence broken only by the hum of insects, the yips of small flying beasts, and the wind across a plain empty of anything they could eat. At the river they turned upstream and traveled a long way across rocky, uneven ground. Gama's knees had begun to ache by the time they reached a place where reeds again flourished, swimmers swam, and small beastlets rustled among the grasses.

Bren raised his hand in the air and the Trontin soumyo waded into the water with their baskets and nets. None of them spoke, but Gama saw the thought-grains moving now and supposed they were think-talking among themselves and to the swimmers, asking the swimmers to give themselves for the soumyo's substance, promising back whatever benefit they had to offer in return for the sacrifice.

Their group waded into the stream as well, shivering at the first bite of cold water against their skins, but they were there for nokif. Gama sang *The Song of Sharing* in her mind, thought-talking it to the reeds—afraid, somehow, that if she sang out loud it might draw the attention of whatever had stolen Frarm.

Each kin stretched out as far from their neighbor as the rope would allow and took out their knives. Gama thanked the reeds for the gift of their bulbs, bent over—her arms in the water almost to her shoulders—and began digging in the sticky mud. She listened hard for a hum while she worked and couldn't help glancing up from time to time, watching for a shimmer in the air. From the corner of her eye she saw others do the same.

But the reeds wouldn't give up their bulbs. No matter how Gama dug around in the mud, on top, underneath, on the sides, the reed held fast to the bulb, and the bulb sucked in hard to the mud.

Frustrated, she stood straight, water dripping off her arms and chest. Her corenta-kin didn't seem to be having any better luck than she had. She looked over at the soumyo from Trontin. Their baskets were practically empty.

She sent a thought-question to the reeds. Plants didn't think in words—they thought in pictures. Sometimes she found it hard to figure out what they were trying to say, but this was easy. The reeds knew what had happened to their vanished brethren further up the stream and for the most part had no intention of giving themselves up to the soumyo—they had their own survival to secure. Gama wiped a wet hand over her face and tried to think of an argument to give the reeds, good reasons why they should sacrifice their bulbs, but couldn't find one. She understood how they felt too well and saw it for what it was—the plants' survival against their empty bellies.

Gama plunged her arms back into the water, grabbed hold of a stalk, and—teeth gritted—yanked it up. Its bulb was large and plump. It would make a good meal.

By the time darkness set in, they had swimmers and bulbs—enough to last a day or two, no more. They'd fought hard for what they had, forced the bulbs from the mud and caught swimmers against their will. It wasn't right, but they were desperate.

The soumyo of Trontin were as wet to the bone as the Reev-kin were, and everyone exhausted from 'the effort. Gama struggled to keep her eyes open. Lifting a foot took nearly all the energy she had left. They trudged back toward the corentas slowly, the heaviness of the air a trick of fatigue.

Slowly she became aware of a hum. She raised her head and looked at the sky. Her heart pounded.

The shimmer was bright, as though the sky had turned to mirror and sunlight glinted off it. She nudged Reln who walked close enough to her that she didn't have to move her elbow far, and looked again to the sky. His gaze followed hers.

Someone behind her screamed. Roped to her kin, Gama could only turn and crane her neck a little ways to look over her shoulder to see what had happened. The soumyo of Trontin, who'd a moment ago walked with them, had vanished. The rope that had connected them lay slack on the ground, their baskets scattered in the dirt.

Males and females together, Gama thought suddenly, remembering what Hest had said. Males and females together, and a disappearance.

Reln, she thought-talked to everyone, not trusting her voice to work. *We can't leave the food here.* It felt wrong to mention the food, petty in comparison to loosing these soumyo, but they couldn't leave it. She reached down and picked up a basket.

Slowly each male and female of Reev and Kelroosh picked up a Trontin basket and added it to their load.

EIGHT

Thought grains floated ahead of Reln—traveling to Trontin, Gama assumed—Reln telling the corenta what had happened. His steps faltered, waiting for a response that was slow in coming. She heard the Kelroosh-kin muttering among themselves, and saw thought-grains moving back and forth between them and among the Reev-kin.

The soumyo are nervous, she sent to Reln. *It might be better to pick up the pace.*

He barely glanced at her. *Get it over with, you mean.*

She shrugged and didn't know if he'd seen her gesture, but he sped his steps and that was good.

-=o=-

They stood shivering in the late-day sun outside the high wall of Trontin corenta—Reln, Prill, the others, and Gama, still lashed together, the rope pulling them closer as it dried. The Kelroosh-kin angled off toward their own corenta, leaving the Reev-kin to make the rest of the short journey to Trontin alone.

I am Reln of Reev, Reln sent to Trontin's soumyo and structures when they reached the wall. *I ask admittance and to speak.*

He stood a long, silent moment. Reln's thought-grains had gone to Trontin, but none returned that Gama saw.

I am Reln, the guide for Reev, he began again.

We know who you are, Trontin's wall sent for all to hear. *You are he who conceived the idea of going outside my protection. The one responsible for the loss of our guide and our kin. Go, Reln of Reev corenta. There is nothing here for you or yours.*

Reln stared at the closed gate. His neck flared gray-red with shock, stunned at the wall's response, Gama thought. A few of his spots lit brown-green in shame. She reached up and touched those spots.

"It's not your fault," she said softly.

It was a fool's argument that Trontin's wall had given. Frarm had vanished from inside Reev. The Trontin kin could have disappeared as easily from inside their corenta as from outside. But the Trontin soumyo and structures were in no mood for logic. They wanted answers, and lacking that, they wanted to place blame. Reln was an easy target.

He stared at her, his lips pressed tightly together, as though caging the words he wanted to say. She felt a few of her spots light purple-gray with concern for him, worry about how the day's happenings had affected him.

"Trontin's wall is right," Reln said, breaking the silence. "It was my idea. Bren didn't like it. I convinced him."

"There was nothing you could have done to save them," Gama said. "You didn't make him or his kin vanish. That's not your doing."

"It'll take a long while for the soumyo of Trontin

to realize that."

He set down the Trontin basket he carried, leaving it for them, and gestured for the others to do the same.

"Can we go to Reev now?" Prill asked, her voice small and fear-filled.

They were all frightened. They all wanted the safety of Reev's wall and closed gates around them, even knowing it offered no real protection at all. Reln nodded, and they practically ran—would have run, if they hadn't still been tied together and everyone afraid of falling, as if a fall would make them vanish too.

-=o=-

Reln paced in the receiving room. If he kept going, Gama thought, he'd wear a hole in the wood floor. Prill had dragged a pillow into a corner and sat with her knees drawn up to her chest, staring at her bare feet.

Gama listened to Wall publically think-talking with the structures at Trontin and Kelroosh. The soumyo and structures of Trontin were in a state. Some wanted to get away from Reev as far and as quickly as possible, but others wanted to stay for what little semblance of security the three corentas standing near each other offered. Final decisions were always left to a corenta's guide, and Trontin had lost theirs. The soumyo in Kelroosh didn't seem to be any more in agreement than those in Trontin.

Oh! Wall sent, though Gama suspected this was

its feeling coming in thought—not meant for the soumyo at all.

The sound outside was loud and unexpected, like thousands of casing-clad feet scraping across dirt—scraping without a let up, a constant din. Gama and Reln looked at each other. Prill shrunk against the wall she leaned on.

They're leaving, Wall sent.

Neither Gama nor Reln asked who—they knew the answer. The scudding changed, become a sound like a storm rising. The dwelling threw open its door and Gama and Reln rushed outside in time to see Trontin corenta lift into the air, heading east. They stood, silent as deadwood, and watched until it was lost in the distance.

When they came back inside, Prill still sat in the corner with her knees pulled up.

NINE

"Reln." Prill stood in the archway between the receiving room and the passageway to the sleeping quarters, her hands clenched together over her stomach. "Reln," she said again, louder this time.

He looked up from the low table where he sat mixing powders. Small clay pots covered the wooden surface, each marked with what was inside. Gama saw his hand stop mid-reach, his eyes focus on Prill.

"I'm leaving, Reln," Prill said.

Reln pulled his hand back to his lap. "Where are you going?"

Prill licked her lips. "With Mahn and Du. To stay in their dwelling."

One spot on Reln's throat flared confusion colors. Prill saw it, and shifted her gaze to Gama and then back to him.

"You're my apprentice," Reln said peaceably. "It will be difficult for us to work together if you stay even a few nights in another dwelling." He gestured to an empty pillow beside him at the table. "Sit now. I'll teach you to mix a poultice to draw out the poison of lenwa bites."

Prill licked her lips again. "I don't want to be your apprentice. Du and Mahn have invited me to learn their weaving ways. I'd rather do that." Her gaze fell to the floor. "I'd rather live with sisters."

Reln set his powders aside. "Reev has many weavers, but only one apprentice healer. You can best serve your kin by staying here and continuing to learn."

"No." Her voice shook, but the only color on her neck was the red-pink of certainty. "I thank you for all you've taught me. That knowledge stays with me and I will use it for my sisters."

She turned and strode down the hall—Reln narrow-eyed, watching the empty space where she'd been, his mouth slightly open and his eyebrow ridges pulled together. Gama opened her mouth to speak, but thought better of it.

Moments later Prill returned, pulling a sled with her personal goods already secured on it. Her eyes focused on the door, not on them. She went straight to it, her steps determined, and stood waiting. The air in the room felt hot, heavy, but the silent thought-grains Prill sent—asking the dwelling to open its door, Gama supposed—moved in their usual way.

The door didn't open.

Prill glared over her shoulder at Reln. They locked gazes, and more silent thought-grains moved through the room, back and forth between Reln and Prill now. Back and forth, and faster and faster. Prill's emotions spots erupted in the dark hues of annoyance and then anger. The thought grains were so thick in the air, Gama was amazed they didn't collide.

Finally Reln threw up his hands. The door flew open and the colors on Prill's throat changed instantly to the red-pink of confidence. She pulled her spine straight and walked out.

Reln stared after her. The door closed. He put his elbows on the table and leaned his face into his palms.

-=o=

Hest. Gama stared into the dimly lit sleeping quarters that days ago held three, but tonight held only her. She watched her thought-grains move through the air, heading toward Home, and waited for a reply.

Hest. Are you awake? Can you hear me?

Nothing.

I miss you, Hest.

-=o=-

Strange noises woke her in the morning. Voices—that was normal enough, though not usually this many, this thunderous—soumyo calling to each other like they were out on the plains or shouting across a river. And a sound she'd never heard before, a sort of lumbering creak, like something huge being dragged through Reev.

Gama sat up and listened harder. Reln had said there was a dim sound before Carding House disappeared. This wasn't muted—it was obvious. She threw her feet over the side of the cot and rushed from the room. How many disappearing structures would it take to make this much noise?

"Reln," she called as she hurried down the hallway toward the receiving room. "Reln!"

Gone out, the dwelling sent, and opened the door. *Go see for yourself.*

The front door swung wide. Gama felt certain that if the dwelling could have pushed her through that opened door, it would have.

She stepped out into chaos.

All the soumyo of Reev, it seemed, were outside, some carrying bags stuffed full, some hauling sleds with their personal property piled on top—clothing, cots and bedding, tables, chests, dishes, floor pillows. A few soumyo moved in packs of three or four, each pack made up of only one gender. As Gama watched, more females or males banded together, each group pointedly not looking at another. The scraping sound grew louder—a sound that set her teeth on edge—but she couldn't see what caused it.

What's going on? she sent to Community Hall, who always seemed to know everything.

A separation and a joining, Hall sent. *You soumyo have gone mad.*

Some structures, too, she sent back, annoyed that Hall seemed to put the chaos only on soumyo shoulders. *Home refused to let Hest and me in, then decided only Hest could be within its walls. Reln's dwelling couldn't get me out its doors fast enough this morning.*

A hot ball grew in her chest as she sent to Hall, remembering how Home had thrown her and Hest out, feeling the rejection again, doubled now that it had taken Hest back, but not her. How Hest had leapt at the offer—leaving her behind. Alone.

Structures, too, Hall agreed. *But more soumyo.*

The scraping and creaking grew louder, its source coming closer. Heads turned in the direction of the noise, most soumyo stopped now, staring, but some looking over their shoulders as they dragged their sleds. The meandering layout of Reev meant they could hear but not see much beyond the structures and commons nearest them.

Then she saw.

They all saw.

Du led a procession of dwellings. A small procession in number—only three—but huge in implication. The structure's broad faces came into view first, sunlight glinting off windows, doors shut, the residences scraping along the ground The dwellings moved slowly through the corenta more gracefully than Gama would have thought they could, They knew, all the soumyo, that structures could move, but if any had ever seen it happen, there were no stories about it. It must have been untold generations since the last structure moved. Why would they? This sort of disharmony was unheard of before now.

Something else stirred in her mind, a memory of a story she'd heard long ago—that just as a full corenta can fly, so can each structure in it, should it choose. These structures had made a different choice, to scrape along slowly, noisily, making a show of it. Whose idea was that—the structures' or Du's?

Du marched ahead, the blue-purple of triumph

glowing on her throat. Gama had a sudden urge to rush out and shove her away, to hold up her hands and force the structures to halt and return to their rightful places through force of will alone. Her neck warmed with equal parts anger and shame colors. Du no longer felt like kin—no true sister would willingly upset their harmony this way—but Du was. She always would be. If the males and females separated, Gama would have Du in the rest of her life, but not Hest, even though they still lived in the same corenta.

Mahn and Prill followed a step or two behind Du, their heads high, blue-purple bright on their throats. Gama tried to catch Prill's eye. Prill looked away.

In places, there wasn't room enough for the dwellings to pass through. Other structures were forced to move back—straining and creaking at the unfamiliar motion—their efforts adding to the growing cacophony. Dust filled the air. A large blue-and-yellow bird suddenly swooped down, flying low over the rooftops, squawking the name they called them, "Gwant. Gwant." The birds usually traveled in pairs, and for half a heartbeat Gama wondered where its mate was.

She'd been focused on the moving structures and hadn't noticed the other females walking beside their dwellings—one with the dwelling that followed Du's, and two more beside the third dwelling—Crina and Tri, who had always lived in it. Were more females walking on the other side, where she couldn't see? There could be none, or the same number, or twice as many. Three times as many. Her stomach clenched.

A group of males stood a small distance from her. They jeered as the dwellings approached, but not loudly, not to make show to any but each other. Gama strained to see if Hest stood with them, and was glad he didn't.

Reln burst through the crowd, took Du by the arm and talked furiously at her, though Gama couldn't hear what he said. The procession skidded to a halt while they spoke, the dwellings behind Du's coming up tight behind it and shifting a little from side to side. The great wind sound of structures talking rose from every direction—an argument, Gama assumed from the depth of blowing. She could guess at what was being said—some saying stay put, others wanting to move. She wondered how many were in harmony with the separation. The structures weren't sharing their thoughts with the soumyo.

From the corner of her eye, she saw the small male band growing restless—craning their necks, glaring at Reln and Du and the soumyo gathered beyond their tight knot. Every throat was lit—anger, fear, and confusion, but some, oddly, showed amusement. She wanted to stomp on those amused feet, change those amusement colors on their throats to the color of despair. Were they without sight? Without compassion? Bit by bit, their lives were being changed. Destroyed. She felt it pressing down, a deep weight in her chest.

This disruption is the males' fault—the thought came

as clear as a voice in her mind. From Reln on out, males didn't understand the importance of staying connected. Of being one. Reln shouldn't have let Prill leave his dwelling. He should have fought for her to stay.

A dark anger coiled in her belly. Males weren't loyal to their sisters. Look how Hest had jumped to go back to Home the moment he was asked. He'd given no thought to her, how she would feel—cast off like a hatchling's down, of no importance in this new life.

Du and Mahn were right. Gama didn't believe it was females and males living together that had brought on the vanishings—didn't believe that separation would end the chaos, the way so many did—but that hardly mattered. Let the males band together for themselves. Let them find their own food, weave their own cloth, and sing their songs with no female voice to add richness.

Her face warmed and her throat burned. Why was she thinking these things, feeling these things? She wanted to shut off the voice in her mind, but the words rolled on. The males had ruined their way of living. They should be shunned, turned out of Reev. Or better—leave Reev to them. A new, clean place for the females would be best.

She looked around at her corenta-kin. Throats that had shown a variety of emotions now all blazed brown-black in anger, the same color she felt on her neck. She couldn't say how she knew, but she was sure the same thoughts that sounded in her mind were being heard in theirs—females blaming males.

The males blaming the females.

Reln gave Du a shove, pushing her away from him. "Open the main gate," he yelled. "These sisters are shunned. They will leave Reev forever." Gama had never seen Reln angry, not like this. She'd never seen him push someone.

Whatever Du felt, it didn't show. How could she feel so little that her neck stayed colorless? She must be feeling deep emotion—anger at Reln, or frustration, something. Du drew her mouth into a tight line, and resumed leading the procession. Mahn stepped up boldly beside her sister. Slowly a color began to glow on both their throats—the red-pink of certainty, the same color Prill had shown when she announced she was leaving. Neither Du nor Mahn had doubts or second thoughts. They believed completely in the rightness of their actions. Whatever was in their minds, whatever goals they sought, felt as true to them as their own names.

Gama looked in the direction of the gate. She couldn't see it from there, but knew it had followed Reln's order and opened. Wall, at least, still listened to Reln.

She didn't know where Du and the other females had thought to go at first, but she didn't think it was out of Reev. More likely to an open space where the three dwellings could sit down close together. Gama felt sure that leaving Reev wasn't what Du had had in mind, but Reln had made his judgment clear. Du was free to do as she wished—outside.

Gama's hand flew to her throat. These females would leave. They would go—where? They had dwellings, but no wall, no protection from the night beasts or from whatever it was that had taken Frarm and the soumyo of Trontin.

Reln, she sent, but he didn't reply. *Reln. These are our sisters. What will happen to them if they leave the protection of Reev? You can still stop this. Please.*

She'd seen the thought-grains float to Reln and be absorbed. Gama knew he'd heard her. He gave silence as his reply.

A female in the crowd stepped into the open way and joined the procession, her head high, and her back as stiff as frozen water.

Another joined.

And another.

Until nearly all the females of Reev were moving together toward the gate.

Despair welled up in her. This was wrong. Females shouldn't leave Reev any more than the males should. They were corenta-kin, female and male together.

Her heart beat against her ribs at a new thought. What would happen to the females who stayed? Would the males throw them out, too—make them *doumanas*—females without males—whether they wanted to be or not?

She huffed out a shaky breath and looked up. The sky shimmered. It was beautiful, as hypnotic as sunlight on moving water. Her sorrow drained away. She wanted to fill her being with that shimmering sky—wanted Hest beside her, so it could fill him too.

This is a day of beauty, she thought. And then

realized it wasn't her thought at all—it was a voice so deep inside that it seemed like her own thought.

All her brothers and sisters stood still, some with heads cocked to the side. Gama knew they heard it too, the voice that seemed like thought. The voice she'd heard in the darkness and then again today telling her that all their troubles were the males' fault.

Don't listen, she sent to her corenta-kin, the thought-grains speeding in all directions.

Her thought-grains reached a sister standing near, came as close to her sister's skin as possible without passing through, then slid away like sand down a hillside. They couldn't hear her.

Thoughts streamed into her head—ideas of a better way of living, a picture in her mind of a giant corenta that didn't move. The deep, peaceful feeling flooded her again. She could see herself living in this new place with her old sisters and with new sisters from other corentas, in tall, just-made dwellings, their every need met. They'd have the chance to do exciting, different sorts of work. Everyone in harmony, content, with no males to disrupt their happiness.

Gama shoved the thought away. It wasn't her thought.

Mahn, Du, Prill, and most of the other females of Reev stood very close together, Du talking fast. The sisters were nodding. Smiles spread on the faces Gama could see.

Prill walked over to her as if in a dream. She reached out and stroked Gama's throat. "Sister," she said, "Du has had a wonderful idea. We females can no longer live in this corenta. We will leave Reev and start a new community, one that's set-placed, in the Gertupa wilderness, far away from the corrupting influences of the males. We'd like you to join us."

Gama saw it clearly in her mind again, the giant corenta with structures taller than any in Reev, gleaming in the sun.

Du and the sisters standing with her eyed Gama with curiosity. She felt heat rising up her breastbone. Had they thought Prill need only stroke her throat and she would follow blindly?

"Prill. This 'thought.' Did it come only to Du, or did all of you think of it at the same time?"

Prill's voice was sure and confident. "The moment Du began to speak, we were in such close harmony we knew what she would say."

Gama rubbed her hands on her thighs, the heat in her chest growing hotter. "What if it wasn't Du's idea at all? What if the thought was fed to her? To all of you. To all of us in Reev."

One of Prill's spots lit with the orange-yellow of confusion. "What do you mean?"

Gama felt her neck warm in response. She was as confused as Prill, trying to pick truth from seemed truth—not sure she knew the difference.

"No matter how close in harmony we are, a whole corenta, females and males, wouldn't have the same thought at the same time unless something was giving us the thought. It's not real. These aren't our visions. They—" She struggled with how to

116

explain what she felt.

Prill's jumped in before she could find the words. "Then whose visions are they?"

"I'm not sure. I just know something is false here. I think something is feeding these thoughts to us, making us do its bidding."

Prill's throat turned nearly all brown-black with anger. "This is the first day in a long time that I haven't been frightened. Today I know I'm going somewhere where life will be good again, peaceful—somewhere I'll be safe."

"But you don't know—"

"Du said you'd be resistant." The dark-brown of disappointment replaced several of the brown-black spots on her throat. "You're tied to Hest. He doesn't want to be your kin anymore. He wants his own life with the males. Making things up and telling tales won't change that."

Her words cut like ice into Gama's heart. There was truth to them, but not whole truth. She was tied to Hest, but her love for him hadn't caused the feeling of wrongness she couldn't shake.

A new vision came to her, of living not in a giant corenta, but in a place where structures stood alone without a wall to embrace them. Gama saw sisters in meadows and fields, gathering crops that offered themselves happily to be food. The same rush of peace she'd felt before filled her again. It was harder to push it away this time. She forced her gaze to the sky, to break the vision.

Gama grabbed Prill's arm. "Look up. That sparkling sky isn't natural. It has something to do with the new thoughts in our minds. We're being led, not traveling in a new direction by free will."

Prill stared at her. Gama kept her face bland. The spots on Prill's neck showed clearly that she feared there was truth in what Gama had said—and that Prill resented her for it. Gama's neck warmed, but it wasn't Prill who caused her anger. She threw her head back.

"Show yourself," she screamed at the sky. "You put words in our minds. Come say them to our faces."

TEN

The sudden and absolute silence stunned her. No whooshing of structures arguing. No voices of her sisters or brothers. She felt the eyes of her kin on her, the heat of her spots warming. The sound of her swallow seemed loud in the silence.

Not complete silence, though—a dim hum vibrated in the background.

Maybe she'd gone mad, but her heart felt true. Her neck erupted with the colors of anger and determination. She turned her gaze back toward the sky, daring whatever was there to show itself. The shimmer shrank in size, then grew dense and brighter.

Du ran toward Prill and Gama, her steps fast and loud. Gama caught Du's movement in the corner of her eye, her focus still on the sky. The glittering bits began to slowly turn. Du grabbed Gama's shoulder and opened her mouth to speak, but Gama shook her head and pointed up. "Look."

The shimmering had formed into wavering bands of gleaming light floating toward them as slowly as leaves through water. The hum grew louder.

Gama's heart pounded like rocks down a hillside. Du's fingers dug into her shoulders.

119

A voice sounded deep inside her—a thrum that filled her whole body.

We have come not to frighten you, something thought-talked, and she saw that all her kin heard and were listening. *We have come to be new with you and better.*

She shot a glance at Reln, expecting him to think-talk back—to speak up for them. He must have realized as she had that the source of this voice and the source of their sorrows was the same. The two had to be connected. The coincidence would be too great if they were not. And there was the hum.

Reln seemed frozen, only the spots on his neck alive with the colors of confusion and fear. Du loosened her grip on Gama's shoulder and hugged her arms over her chest. Gama's glance sped from face to face. All her kin seemed struck dumb and frozen where they stood, except Prill, who looked ready to run. Gama touched her throat gently, worried that if Prill panicked, everyone would.

Who are you? Gama sent.

Prill pulled away, but stood still, listening now, the corner of her bottom lip caught between her teeth.

A sparkling band wavered in front them. Du reached out to touch the thing. Gama grabbed her hand and pulled it back. Du looked at her, a bit wild-eyed. The band grew bright—brighter.

I, in particular, am called Weast, the voice said. *I speak for the us. We all together are the lumani. Our home is far from here. We have traveled and seen you and watched. We apologize for confusion we may have caused through no fault of us.*

Prill blinked, as if just waking from a deep sleep and surprised to find herself standing there.

Other bands floated above their heads. Gama tried to count them, but the shapes shifted and moved so much that it was impossible. Around them the sky was a vivid blue and cloudless.

Gama glared at Reln again, wanting him to act, to communicate with whatever this was hanging before them in the air. Her heart pounded. She put her hand over her throat to hide the fear colors there, in case these sparkling things could read them and see how deep her fear ran.

Why have you come? she sent to the sparkling thing that named itself Weast. *What do you want?*

To improve you and watch, it sent. *To be not kin, but friends with kind gifts of a better life.*

The giant corenta, she sent, sure now that these things—these lumani—had delivered the pictures to the soumyo's minds. What did Weast mean by *to improve you?*

Prill stood next to Gama, her eyes darting from side to side as she listened. Gama touched her neck again and gave her a thin smile. Prill smiled back, but the smile was strained. Color flared on Prill's throat as panic rose in her again.

The picture came once more, the giant corenta, filling Gama's mind. The sense of peace the picture brought chilled her. It worked on Prill. Her smile broadened and became real. Her muscles relaxed. The colors on her throat changed from muddy-brown to the pale-green of contentment.

Gama gave up covering her throat—if the lumani could read the colors, they already knew what each soumyo felt. She put her hand to her forehead instead, to shade her eyes from the brightness of the glittering bands.

What sort of better life are you offering? she asked Weast.

A pleasant one. Open space for making food so there will never be hunger. Places for processing a mineral we have seen here that will give new ease to your living. Places for males and places for females, where each may find joy. We have many gifts for you.

Again the mind-pictures came, a corenta without a wall, set down by a verdant meadow. And again, the rush of peace.

The pale-green of contentment grew brighter on Prill's throat, joined by the silver-blue of gratitude. Du's throat showed the same.

Pale-green and silver-blue in various intensities and combinations glowed on nearly every throat Gama could see. Here and there the pale-yellow-blue of acceptance, or the brown-black of anger, or the muddy-brown of fear. She felt her own fear rising—fear of this feeling of peace. Fear of the lumani.

Her gaze stopped again at Reln. Why didn't he speak up? Interrupt her think-talk with his own and take over? He was their guide. This was his duty.

Their eyes met. Reln looked away—and Gama saw the reason as clearly as sand through clean water. All that had happened, the vanishings, the corenta that wouldn't let him in, disharmony in

Reev, Prill leaving to be with her sisters—it had shattered his heart and left him broken.

Her mind spun. She wanted Hest beside her—Hest, whose presence made her feel smarter and more capable. Hest, who had walked away, leaving her alone. She wanted Hest but didn't need him. Didn't need anyone but herself.

This sparkling thing was an intelligence, she was sure. Different, but no more different from the soumyo than the structures or the plants. Unless what they saw was not the intelligence itself, but its agent. Did that matter? Somewhere an intelligence, a life force, had come into the world and created chaos. Now it offered a solution—a new way of living.

Why?

She thought-talked the question publically. Prill sent her a sharp look, as though afraid questions might drive away the lumani and the promised peaceful life.

We wish to learn, Weast sent. *You have much to teach us.*

What could they possibly teach these creatures that came from the sky and could plant thoughts in their minds? She could come back to that. There was another question that bothered her more. *When will you leave?*

The band that was Weast drew in on itself, contracting to a small ball of light.

Of sorrow, Weast sent, *we came but cannot leave again. Our corentas—as you would name them—are destroyed and cannot move. We will never be among those we love again.*

Today we seek to give gifts and live among those of this place forever more.

Sometimes a seed blows away from the plant and grows in a new place. Sometimes that new plant blocks out the sun from what grew there before. Gama didn't like the thought that these lumani were here for good. Who could say if Weast was telling the truth about being stuck here, or if it was a convenient lie? Du and Prill seemed delighted with the idea of the lumani staying, to judge by the colors on their necks.

Reln suddenly found his voice. *Came from where?* he thought-talked.

Weast gave no answer. The glittering ball slowly rotated, then stretched out again into a band. Prill hugged her arms across her stomach, but the colors on her throat didn't change.

We wish to speak with only one, Weast finally sent, *as we speak through only one. This makes for clarity.*

Relief was in Reln's voice when he spoke. "Gama, please continue."

A privilege she didn't particularly want. She swallowed hard, and found herself looking for Hest—again wanting him beside her. He was there, somewhere in the crowd, but she couldn't find him. Gama turned her attention back to Weast. *Where is the place you came from?*

The glimmering bits contracted into a straight line that angled west of the sun. *Our place is there, but past the sky.*

Her hands felt sweaty. She rubbed them against her hipwrap. Creatures from the sky, wanting to change the way the way the soumyo lived, calling it a gift. The soumyo had no word for what Gama feared: that these creatures would take more than they gave. Why didn't the corenta-kin see the danger, the falseness of Weast's words?

"Tell them," Reln said, breaking into her thoughts, "'You've given us much to think and talk about. We need time alone to discuss it.'"

She stared at him a moment, her heart shaking in her chest, then sent, *Did you take our kin? The beasts, and birds, and structures, and our kin—it was you?*

"Gama," Reln said, his voice low.

The sparkling line began to curl on itself, forming a disk. Gama tried to figure out if the motions meant something, but they seemed pointless—or beyond her understanding.

We wish to learn of this place, Weast sent. *To learn we must closely examine. We were not of the knowledge that some were thinking creatures until we did examine. We will not take more of this kind.*

"We're safe now," Du whispered to Prill.

Gama swung her head and glared a moment at her two sisters. Her chest felt tight. She pushed aside her disgust with Du and turned her focus back to the lumani. Gama thought-talked the question that had scratched at her mind from the first moment Weast had spoken. *Will you return what was taken?*

The disk of Weast began to slowly turn. *What no longer exists cannot be brought back.*

Reln closed his hand around her arm. "I need time. I need... We..." His grip tightened. "Say what

I told you."

Gama's mind felt numb. She couldn't remember what Reln wanted her to say. Frarm, their brother, was destroyed. The soumyo of Trontin—gone. The kin stood listening, a mix of colors on every throat. Iya showed the muddy-yellow of indignation. Gama took comfort in that—felt less alone.

Reln's hand tightened on her arm and the words flooded back to her. *You've given us much to think and talk about. We need time alone to discuss it.*

Slowly the band that called itself Weast began to break apart, the sparkling bits rising to join the ones over their heads.

We will go, Weast sent, *and come again soonest for your answer.*

Reln said nothing as he turned and headed toward Community Hall.

ELEVEN

The plaster-clad stone and mortar walls of Community Hall felt hard but reassuring behind Gama's back. Chatter was loud in the room, and thought-grains floated in every direction. The females and the males had separated themselves—each to their own side, each talking only with sisters or brothers. Gama stayed silent. Words were too heavy. They sank in her throat.

She craned her neck looking for Hest. He had to be there. Every soumyo of Reev was there. The female-and-structure departure had stopped after the thing that called itself Weast had spoken, the roving dwellings still waiting where they had halted when the sky began to shimmer.

Hest, she sent and watched the thought-grains travel through the room, finding their target. He stood in a corner, alone. She knew he'd heard her, had seen the thought-grains reach his skin and pass through. It must have been the lumani that stopped the grains from passing through before. Hest's back tensed and he sucked in a breath, but didn't acknowledge her. Gama stared at him—the sting of his rejection as sharp as a bite.

A group of three males made its way to him, chattering in his direction. Hest joined the conversation as though it might save his life.

Gama picked up the tumbler of heated zwas that sat next to her on the floor and wrapped her hands around it. The warmth seeped into her palms and fingers. She stared unseeing into the bright red liquid, then set the tumbler down without drinking.

When she looked up, Prill stood in front of her, a smile on her face.

"It's exciting, don't you think?" Prill dropped a blue floor pillow next to where Gama sat and settled herself cross-legged on it. "A set place to live. High walls to protect us. No more worrying about what might disappear next—who might vanish." A shiver ran across Prill's shoulders. "We'll be safe. Safe and happy."

Gama shifted her gaze away. They would trade everything for safety, even the illusion of it.

Prill touched Gama's throat. "While you've been with us, living with Reln and me, I've come to feel close to you. You're more adventurous than I am. I'm more sensible than you are. We make a good balance. I hope you'll be happy in our new set-place corenta."

Why did Prill assume she'd go with the doumanas? That was the last thing she wanted to do. Gama spotted Reln threading his way through the crowd toward the dais. She nudged Prill and pointed her chin toward their guide.

Prill rubbed her mouth with her hand and leaned against the wall, watching. "What do you think he'll say?"

Gama shrugged. Nothing was what she thought

anymore—the world turned upside down and spiky. She couldn't predict anything that might happen.

Reln climbed onto the dais and spread his arms wide in sign that he would speak. The soumyo didn't quiet quickly. Their respect for their guide was fading, Gama realized. This was his moment— his chance to say the right words to stop the split between female and male and hold Reev corenta together. She leaned forward.

Reln looked out over the kin of Reev, opened his mouth, but no words came out.

The hall had gone silent, the kin waiting, some growing restless, shifting from hip to hip, or rearranging their legs. Reln drew in a deep breath. Gama felt her neck warm, wanting him to make sense from the madness. He opened his mouth again, then shut it. The pale-blue of despair bloomed on his throat.

Du jumped to her feet. "Maybe Reln has nothing to say, but I do." She strode through the hall and climbed onto the dais—a breach of manners that would have been shocking before today.

Gama stared at her sisters and brothers. No one seemed offended. No one even seemed surprised. They simply waited to hear what Du would say. Prill's neck lit with anticipation colors. Gama's head began to throb.

"I speak to my sisters of Reev." Du's voice rang through the hall. "A grand opportunity has been offered to us—the chance to make a new life, free from the males, who have shown themselves to be unfaithful members of the kin. They have shirked their work and think only of their own wellbeing above and before the good of the corenta."

Males around the room noised their feelings about that, the few throats Gama could see lighting gray-green in disgust or muddy-yellow with indignation. But females leaned forward and nodded.

Did they not see that the lumani had forced these thoughts into the soumyo's heads? The orange-red on Prill's neck grew brighter. Gama put a hand to the side of her face, to block out sight of those colors.

Du turned and looked a long moment at Reln, then faced the corenta-kin again. "Mahn and I have accepted the opportunity offered us by the sky-dwellers. We invite our sisters to join us, not only our sisters here in Reev, but from Kelroosh, and all corentas. Together, in a green meadow beyond the hills, we will build a new, stable corenta. We will make a fresh life, free from worry and want. We will find new opportunities, new ways of living, and new freedoms."

Gama lowered her hand, looked at Prill and tried to find words, but none came. They had given in so easily—her sisters and brothers—to this idea: the stable corenta. That new place Du spoke of could never be a corenta. Movement was the essence of Reev, of Kelroosh, of all corentas. Whatever that new place would be, it couldn't be called by the old name—it would need something new.

New ways of living, new freedoms, Du had

said—as the lumani promised. Everything new and safe and wonderful—the lumani's gifts. The kin ran to it like thirsty brez to a waterhole. Anything, Gama supposed, to stop the chaos, even if it meant convincing yourself that this new life was exactly what you wanted.

"Sisters," Du said. "I invite all who wish to join us in the great adventure to stand."

Prill pulled to her feet, almost kicking Gama in her haste. All through their half of the hall, females were standing, some quickly, though some with hesitation. Gama peered through the thicket of legs. Only three sisters remained seated, Iya, among them. Gama hoped there were more she couldn't see in the crowded hall, or that some who stood now might change their minds, but judging from the colors alight on every throat, that didn't seem likely. Her heart sank.

Du's neck turned nearly white with satisfaction.

"Come, my sisters," she said. "Let us go now and prepare for our departure. Speak to your dwellings. All who wish to join us, may. Tomorrow we set out from Reev to begin new and wondrous lives."

The sisters headed toward the doors of Community Hall. They stroked each other's brightly lit throats and walked with the sure steps of those confident in their choices.

Gama felt her own neck warm, her spots turning blue-red with anxiety. How could her sisters believe the lumani's promises? Creatures that took their kin before their eyes couldn't be trusted. Why didn't the kin see that? Why didn't Reln speak out? Warn them. Talk sense.

Why didn't she?

Gama rubbed her hands across her thighs. Maybe she was wrong in her choice. She should join her sisters.

There was something false about the lumani— she felt it in her depths.

"Sisters!" Gama called, pulling herself to her feet. "Wait."

Only a few heads turned to look in her direction.

Remember Frarm, and the soumyo of Trontin, Gama thought-talked to the room. *Think of the chaos the lumani caused. Why would they now suddenly be concerned for us, our welfare? Don't listen to their words. Listen to your heart.*

Most of her sisters couldn't have cared less what she'd said. They sent no thoughts back, didn't even turn her way to look. One sister who hadn't risen with the others stood now. Confusion colors were on her throat. She wanted to speak, Gama knew she did, but fear or indecision had stopped her. She sat again, then stood and moved toward Du and the others.

Vonti climbed onto the dais and waved his arms.

"Brothers," he called out. "I, too, am accepting the lumani's offer. They have shown me the future. Our males' stable corenta will be built alongside a wide river full of swimmers. We will dance and make music, our every need provided for. Who will come with me?"

Kis stood. "I will." He made his way across the floor to stand below Vonti. Other males stood and followed.

Hest stood with them.

No, she thought-talked to him. *Please, Hest. Don't go with Vonti. Stay in Reev. Stay yourself.*

I am myself, Hest sent back, the first words they'd had since he'd walked away from her and moved back into Home. *I've considered it carefully. I've made the right choice. I wish you were male, Gama—we'd never be parted.*

His thoughts were like a blow, driving the air from her lungs. She couldn't gather breath to replace it.

From the back of Community Hall, Fel called out, "I stand with Reev. I'll not leave my corenta for some vague promise. Who stands with me for Reev?"

A few males made their way through the crowd to Fel, a handful, no more. Gama saw Hest rub the bottom of his face, thinking.

Her heart leapt up. If Hest would stay—

She wanted to think-talk to him, to build a case, give him every reason why he should stay. She had arguments in mind and emotional pleas she could offer, but she stayed silent. It was his decision to make.

Hest stood a long moment, as still as a lone boulder in a meadow. Gama caught the movement of his eyes as his gaze slid toward her, and then away. He licked his lips and took a step, walking toward the dais, toward those who would leave Reev forever.

-=o=-

Gama tossed restlessly in the dark on the cot in Reln's dwelling—Hest gone, Prill gone, not even Reln in his own dwelling. She thought-talked toward Reev's guide, asked where he was, when he'd be returning. If he heard her—he must have heard her—he chose not to answer.

It seemed she'd barely fallen asleep when Reln's dwelling woke her. The morning light was weak through the windows, as though the sun itself didn't want this day to come.

We'll be rising, the dwelling sent. *Best get ready.*

She scrubbed her eyes with the back of her fists. "Where are we going?" she said aloud, just to hear a spoken voice in this silent place.

Nowhere. Only rising, to let the structures out who wish to leave.

"The dwellings left yesterday with those who believe the lumani," she said, her mind still foggy.

Other structures also wish to leave. Some are too large to fit through Wall's gate. We will lift toward the sky. Those who wish to abandon us will go. You can stand at the door if you want to watch.

She heard the slight bang as the door swung open hard and hit the outside wall. Gama walked slowly down the hall and through the receiving room, in no hurry to see more of the desertion of Reev but needing to witness it. She held tight to the jamb as Reev shook itself free of the land and lifted into the air. Iya stood in a nearby doorway, watching too. She raised a hand to Gama in sad greeting. Gama gave her a small smile in return, glad that Iya had chosen to stay. At least she'd have one sister in

Reev.

The structures were talking in their own speech, the wind-sound of their voices adding to the true wind passing by Gama's ears as Reev slowly left the land behind, no different than any other time Reev had lifted off, except now she wasn't secured behind a shut door and could see how the sky seemed to come closer as they rose. She heard the creaking of the structures and their voices blowing through Reev. Her stomach felt queasy.

She braced herself between the jambs, closed her eyes, and thought about the word Reln's dwelling had used: abandon.

You're sad, aren't you?

Mourning. My friends are leaving. Structures that have been here as long as I have, or newer friends, built recently. When will I see them again? Maybe never.

She wished the dwelling had a throat, so she could stroke it. She rubbed the jamb, hoping the touch would bring it some comfort, and sent, *Many of us are sad today.*

Yes, the dwelling sent. *I fear those that are happy now will find themselves sorrowful in a distant tomorrow.*

Gama let out a sigh. *And that by then it will be too late.*

When she opened her eyes again, she saw that Reev had risen higher than the tallest structure and now hovered in the air. The thin soil crackled as the grains began to separate. Dust spiraled in the air. The dwelling across from where she stood slowly sank through the loosened soil, disappearing hand-span by hand-span from her sight, the way a drowned beast sinks beneath the water. It landed with a soft crash. A structure-shaped hole gaped wide where it had stood, the dark soil of the meadow visible beneath it. The hole lasted only moments. Then the soil moved and covered the emptiness.

When all the structures that wanted to leave had sunk away, Reev slowly moved sideways and then settled itself back onto the ground.

Females and males rushed from Community Hall and the communiteria, and from dwellings that had chosen to stay. It was only then she realized the departing structures had been empty of soumyo when they'd dropped through the soil. Vonti, Kis, and others pulled sleds with their belongings tied on securely. She stepped out to the path's edge and watched them go.

No one looked at her as they passed. Females called to their sisters, males to their brothers, and they joined in packs, heading toward the gates. Gama followed a female group a while, trailing like a hatchling, invisible, forgotten in its slowness.

Wall had thrown open the gate. Soumyo pushed at each other and elbowed their way to be first or next in line. The soft-gray of sorrow burned on Gama's throat. When she couldn't watch any longer, she turned and wandered through Reev, passing open space after open space where yesterday her corenta-kin had laughed and lived in harmony, and been part of a community.

She returned to Reln's dwelling alone.

-=o=-

Reln is coming, the dwelling sent.

Gama pulled to her feet. She hadn't seen or spoken with Reln since he'd failed to speak in Community Hall. She hurried to the receiving room, anxious to talk with him and hear his plans for those remaining in Reev. Their number would be smaller now. Work allotments would have to be changed. Some among them would need to master new skills.

He's not alone, the dwelling sent. *Several are with him. We've talked it and talked it. It must be done, Gama. I am sorry.*

She slowed her steps, her neck warming. *What—*

The dwelling opened its door before she could finish the question. Reln and five males who'd chosen to stay stood just beyond the threshold. Gama's gaze shot to their throats, to gauge what sort of message might be coming. Reln's spots were lit purple-gray—he was worried, concerned, but the others felt differently—their throats splotched gray-green in disgust and ocher with impatience. She put her hand over her own throat to hide the anxiety colors she knew glowed there.

"I'm sorry, Gama," Reln said. "This is no longer a place for you."

Confused, she dropped her hands to her sides and stared at him. She'd thought they'd grown close in harmony lately. She'd thought this dwelling would shelter her. Hadn't Reln and it each said as much? Reln saw the colors on her throat and knew she was anxious and confused, but offered no words to comfort her. Gama barely kept her voice from shaking. "Home is gone, left with Hest. If you don't want me here, maybe Community Hall will take me in."

"No," Reln said, his voice firm. "Not Community Hall. Not anywhere in Reev."

A chill raced up her breastbone. "What are you saying?"

"Reev will no longer shelter you or any female." Reln's voice softened. "It was a hard decision, Gama, but given all that's happened, we few who remain as part of Reev feel it's best that we be an all male corenta. Wall agrees, and Community Hall, the granaries—all of the remaining structures, in fact."

Do you? she sent privately to Reln's dwelling. *You've been kind since the night Hest and I first came to stay.*

I, too, am sorry, Gama. It was not an easy decision. The lumani returned in the night and spoke with Reln. They want male and female separated. If all the females are gone, the sky-creatures have promised to leave Reev alone. Best for us all if you go.

She looked at the males standing with Reln. Each now showed the color of determination on his throat. There was no point in arguing, in trying to convince Reln that this separation was a scheme devised by the lumani for reasons of their own, like everything else the sky-creatures had done.

Reln took a half step toward her. She hoped he would reach out and stroke her throat, offer some comfort at least, but he didn't.

"Reev has spoken with Kelroosh," he said. "They have eight males who've chosen to stay, and about twenty or so females. Their males will come here. You and the other Reev females who've stayed may go to Kelroosh if you wish."

The shaking started in her arms, spread through her chest, and sped down her legs. Moments passed and she couldn't speak. She huffed, trying to get the air needed to force out speech, and then, the words flew from her mouth. "If I wish? Where else would I go, Reln? Out by myself beside some stream? Maybe you think I could walk far enough to find an unclaimed orchard to call my own? That by myself I could build a dwelling before some beast found me? There's no 'If I wish' here. No choice at all."

Her gaze flew from male face to male face— throat to throat. Reev was home. She'd emerged here, lived here all her years. She couldn't leave.

"It's for the best, Gama," Reln said. "In time, you will see this is our way forward."

I doubt that, she thought-talked to Reln, and said aloud, "Can I at least gather my goods? Or would you send me to Kelroosh with only the hipwrap I'm wearing and nothing else?"

"Of course." Reln rubbed his hand over his scalp. "A sled will be brought. Your sisters are packing as well. You can meet them at the gate."

She looked at him a long moment, then turned and went to get her things.

-=o=-

She went to the small communiteria first and wrapped her cooking pots, personal bowls, tumblers, and spoons in a cloak she found hanging there—Prill's. Gama supposed Prill didn't want it anymore. Maybe Prill thought the lumani would hand out new ones. What was it Vonti had said? The lumani would provide for their every need.

The room she'd shared with Hest and Prill was nearly empty now. Hest had taken everything that was his, as had Prill. It took little time to gather her hipwraps, foot casings, and cloaks. The tiny, misshapen bowl Hest had made from clay they'd dug one day on a riverbank sat in its spot near the head of her cot. Gama stared at it a long moment, then wrapped it separately in its own hipwrap—layers to keep it safe.

When she returned to the receiving room only Reln was there, an empty sled next to him. They didn't speak while she loaded her things, Reln watching but not offering to help. She knotted the rope that secured her goods to the sled tightly, stood, and looked at him, needing to say something—needing to hear him say something. Reln shook his head and pressed his lips in a tight line.

Gama nodded, picked up the sled's rope, and headed for the door.

Iya was already at the gate when Gama arrived, and two older females she didn't know well. There was no need to speak—their necks showed their despair. Why waste words when they could see everyone felt the same?

Wall swung open the gate and they passed through, heading for Kelroosh, anchored a short distance away.

In the space between the two corentas, Kelroosh's males, pulling sleds of their own, headed toward Reev. When the males grew near, Gama looked away, to not witness the pale-blue of despair on their throats—flaming as brightly as she knew her own spots glowed.

She turned her head and peered over her shoulder one last time at Reev, her home, the place where she'd been happy. Where she had loved and been loved. *Hest*, she thought, and felt the loss like a hole blown through her—sure that anyone who looked could see it.

She tightened her grip around her sled's rope pull. She didn't want it—this despair and surrender. She eased close to Iya and put her free arm over her sister's shoulders. Iya slid her free arm around Gama's waist. They matched their pace and walked in harmony, their steps stronger together.

A few females stood outside Kelroosh, waiting to greet the new arrivals. Gama looked up at the high, thick wall, at the large wooden gate, weathered but strong, that had opened to receive them.

"This is a day of sorrow and joy," Kinto, Kelroosh's guide, said as Gama and her sisters passed into the corenta.

Gama slowed her step. She should say something, thank Kinto for taking them in. She tried, but nothing seemed right. Kinto reached out and stroked her throat.

The touch calmed and reassured Gama. She stood and looked around, Iya doing the same next to her. Kelroosh was bigger than Reev and many of its dwellings had left too, leaving large spaces of bare dirt between structures. So many spaces, so many of the kin gone.

"The sorrow," Kinto said.

Gama nodded. Hest was her sorrow—smaller than Kinto's loss, but no less painful.

-=o=-

"The joy," Kinto said, "is you and your sisters, whom we have gained."

Gama breathed out long and loud, taking in as much as she could see of Kelroosh from that spot: brightly painted structures she guessed were dwellings, a large commons, a round dun-colored structure that might be a grain house, and in the distance what was likely their community hall. She saw the possibilities now—new dwellings built, new sisters loved. These females, the few of Reev and Kelroosh who would not believe the lumani's false promises, who would not trade their way of life for safety, they were her new kin. She'd make a new life with them.

They would go forward together.

Acknowledgments

Many thanks to Dan McNeil, Meg Xuemei, Randy Jackson, Richard Casey, and Sue Marschner, wonderful writers all, for their help in shaping this story. Special thanks to Christina Frey and Jay Howard, the best editors a writer could hope for.

Much love to Chris, Colin, and Larkin Razevich, who make every day a joy.

Cover art by Tony Honkawa, Tony Honkawa Design

About the Author

Alexes Razevich was born in New York and grew up in Orange County, California. She attended California State University San Francisco where she earned a degree in Creative Writing. After a successful career on the fringe of the electronics industry, including stints as Director of Marketing for a major trade show management company and as an editor for Electronic Engineering Times, she returned to her first love—fiction. She lives in Southern California with her husband. When she isn't writing, she can usually be found playing hockey or traveling somewhere she hasn't been before.

Alexes is always happy to hear from readers and welcomes new friends on Facebook and Twitter.

Email: LxsRaz@yahoo.com

Twitter: https://twitter.com/lxsraz

Facebook:
https://www.facebook.com/AlexesRazevichAuthor

New Release Mailing List:
ttp://eepurl.com/08229

Website: http://www.alexesrazevich.com/

SHADOWLINE DRIFT Sample

ONE

Heat and dirt. Air like molasses. Eighty degrees, but it was early still. One hundred and fifty feet from his tent to the hut, though it seemed further in the hot, wet air. Jake was good at that sort of thing—figuring out temperatures, people's height and age, the desires of their secret hearts.

From habit, he checked his watch—half past seven—and rubbed the titanium-cased face for luck. The watch had been a gift from his parents on his thirtieth birthday. It was much too nice and certainly too expensive, and a bit too big for his size, but then, wasn't everything? He'd been embarrassed by their generosity, but pleased with the gift. In the three years since, it'd been a lot of places with him, some of them dicey, and he'd grown superstitious—as long as he wore the watch, he'd come home safe and successful. Safety mattered in the backwaters of the Amazon, but success this trip was critical. He drew a breath and stepped into the palm-sided hut occupied by the man he'd come a long way to see.

The hut felt dark inside after the bright sun. Dust motes hung in the still air, caught in the thin shaft of light streaming through a small slit in the wall opposite the door. The man, Mawgis, sat cross-legged on a thick, woven-leaf mat. An identical mat lay across from him. Beneath the mat, the packed-dirt floor was a brown so deep it was nearly black. A pile of small stones lay near Mawgis, and nothing else, so it wasn't living quarters. A place for gatherings? It struck him as odd. Why would the Tabna, a small tribe of twenty-seven people, need a building just for that? Unless a bedroll was stashed out back. That was possible. He'd been well briefed for this meeting, but the briefings had focused on what someone else thought he should know, not the small things he might wonder about.

Mawgis squinted up at him, appraising. "Not very tall, are you?"

The man's voice was rich and deep, a bow drawn slowly across cello strings, Hebrew or Gaelic sounding. The raisin-sized translator nestled in Jake's ear droned, sorting language from the background noise of calling birds and nattering monkeys.

"Three and a half feet," Jake said, knowing the measurement had no meaning for the Tabna man.

"About the same height as you."

The older man was thin and wiry, and though Mawgis calmly sat, Jake felt an electric energy in him. His face was interesting: golden-brown skin barely wrinkled with age, and loam-colored eyes. High cheekbones. Broad nose and thin-lipped mouth. Three precise rows of vertical scars on each cheek—the scars rubbed with yellow dye. The man's features went together so well, he seemed more drawn by an artist's hand than something natural-born.

Jake felt Mawgis inventory him in return, the man's eyes flickering over him. Blue shirt, khaki shorts, leather hiking boots. Dusty-brown hair—longish. Blue-gray eyes. Sunburned skin, glazed with perspiration. Jake certainly didn't look like the Salesian missionaries who'd discovered the previously unknown tribe, each priest tall and dark of skin, hair, and eyes. He wondered what Mawgis made of him, of all of them—the five pale men and one brown man who'd come to see him now, each for his own reasons.

Mawgis ran a knuckle across one of the scars on his right cheek and adjusted the blue and red parrot feather circlet at his neck. Other than the feathers, he wore only a leaf folded around his penis. The Amazonian humidity had plastered Jake's shorts and shirt to his body like an ill-fitting skin. He resisted the urge to pull the fabric away.

Mawgis glanced at the empty mat across from where he sat, indicating that Jake should sit. He cleared his throat. "How was your journey?"

"Difficult," Jake said, settling onto the mat and crossing his legs into a loose pretzel form that mirrored his host's. "We traveled the Amazon and the Japurá Rivers, then branched off to a tributary with terrible rapids. One boat turned over. No one was hurt, but we lost supplies and equipment. We hiked six days through the forest with our gear on our backs to reach you."

The older man gazed at him. "You've been other places?" he asked, making no comment on the ordeal.

"Many," Jake said.

Banshees screamed in the trees—howler monkeys. It was hardly the first time Jake had heard them, but the sound still made his shoulders tense.

Mawgis tapped his chest. "I, too, am greatly traveled."

Jake nodded and kept his face blank. Well-traveled was a matter of perspective.

The other man swept up a pile of pea-sized stones from near his feet. "When were you born?" The stones in his hands rattled softly—a sound like dry grass hissing in the wind.

"I'm thirty-three." He knew it was a meaningless answer. The Tabna had no concept of the 365-day cycle of the earth around the sun. They reckoned time by events—when the ants left their nests to forage, when the rains stopped, when the jaguar ate the old chief. That's what he'd been told by Father Canas, the missionary who had spent eighteen months living with the Tabna, compiling a Tabna-English dictionary. Last month he'd helped Jake prepare for this job.

Mawgis touched the translator in his left ear. "You misunderstand," he said. A small yellow ant crawled up his leg and he squashed it between his thumb and forefinger. "I ask—when did you leave the womb?"

Jake tried to figure a way to answer, but came up with nothing.

The older man peeked at the stones in his hands. A quick smile lit his face—bright white teeth, the middle two a little long. "You were born when your chief first walked in his new house, though it wasn't his then."

Jake silently cursed Father Canas, who'd assured him the English translations were at least ninety-seven percent accurate. They were going to have a hard time doing business if their words continued to be scrambled.

"Delacort," Mawgis said, the stones clicking in his hands. "Present Delacort."

He seemed so sure of himself; Jake tried to make sense of it.

Jesus. *President* Delacort. Jake had indeed been born the year Jonathan Delacort, as a newly elected senator, first arrived in Washington. Now in his late sixties, Delacort was president.

Jake bent his mouth in the smallest of smiles. Better to let Mawgis think him amused, not surprised. "Yes. How did you know?"

The Indian's eyes slid away from Jake.

The morning mist turned into a sudden shower—fat raindrops falling like dotted lines outside the hut's open doorway, thudding against the palm-thatched roof. Something—Jake saw only a flash of rat-like tail—skittered above the hut's simple tree-branch framing, through the palm fronds overhead. He waited.

Mawgis opened his hands and held out the stones. "Choose two."

A dozen or so pebbles of various colors, some speckled and some solid brown, white, or black, rested in his cupped hands. Jake chose one white and one gray-speckled. Mawgis closed his fingers over the remaining stones, chanted a few words that came through the translator as static, and threw the pebbles on the ground between them.

On a job in Haiti, Jake had watched a thin, bumpy-spined woman read chicken entrails, bent over so far that her nose practically touched the offal, her eyes being not as sharp as they'd once been. Mawgis wore the same concentrating yet confident look as he studied the pebbles, though his spine was straight, his shoulders down and relaxed.

"What do the stones tell you?" Not that Jake believed a handful of gravel had told Mawgis the year he had been born or had given the man a context in which to express the time. Not that he thought any significance lay in which two stones he'd chosen. What Jake wanted to know was this: what did Mawgis want to tell him?

"The stones?" Mawgis said, and blinked slowly, like a turtle. The blink didn't go with the feeling of pent-up energy Jake sensed in him. "That you are a plain man. More clever than you like people to know, and resolute. You will fight to the end for what you believe is right."

A moment passed, the ever-present noise of the forest leaping into the silence. Mawgis shook his head as if trying to clear his thoughts. "Follow," he said, stood, and headed out the door.

Jake walked out behind him, thinking that the description Mawgis had given for him could fit any number of people. Thinking, too, that he had no more idea now what Mawgis wanted him to know than when he'd awoken that morning in the yellow canvas tent he'd hurriedly pitched the night before. He'd finally made it to his destination only to discover that the man he'd come to see was out in the forest somewhere.

The rain stopped as quickly as it had begun, leaving the air so thick with moisture Jake felt he almost could have rolled it between his hands and formed a solid ball. He peered through the wet haze at the Tabna camp. His mind had been on his meeting with Mawgis when he'd come through the camp that morning. He hadn't paid much attention to his surroundings. But these things mattered—appreciating where and how people lived, being friendly to and getting to know the people around the decision maker. A perk of the job, in Jake's opinion.

Spaced around the camp's perimeter were eleven palm-sided huts the same size and shape as the one Mawgis and Jake had left. The thatched roofs were A-shaped, with wide eaves to let the rain slide off. Vine-woven hammocks hung between poles set in front of the huts. Some were in use, their occupants swinging contentedly. The people must have all been inside while the rain fell. None of them were wet.

Three canvas tents were set up near the camp's perimeter, Jake's and the two used by the men who'd accompanied him on this trip—four Brits making a documentary about the Tabna, and Joaquin Machado from FUNAI, the Brazilian government office charged with protecting the rights of indigenous people. The film crew's four-man tents were about the same size as the Tabna huts. Jake's tent, big enough for two normal-sized adults, was smaller than the huts but spacious for him.

A young Tabna woman—Jake guessed her to be fifteen, sixteen at most—swayed lazily in a hammock, one slim brown leg hanging over the edge. Small white dots covered her shoulders and upper arms like a shawl. Her thick, straight black hair was cut short, like Mawgis's. Her breasts were small and firm. She eyed Jake and smiled. He smiled back.

Birds called in the jungle now that the rain had stopped, every throat proclaiming its own loud and raucous song. Gnats as small as grains of salt whirled near Jake's head. He batted them away and tried to come up even with Mawgis, but no matter how fast he walked, the older man stayed half a step ahead.

In the large central area where the communal socializing, cooking, and eating took place, two

Tabna men were showing a group of boys how to make spears. Ian, one of the British film crew, had his camera trained on a child struggling to attach a spear tip to the shaft. The boy looked up at the camera and grinned. Jake wondered what the Tabna thought about all the sudden attention they were receiving.

Mawgis led him toward the smoke and then past the big iron cauldron that served as the community cooking pot. A dozen men and women worked at preparing the evening meal, which was, Jake saw, going to be termites, squirrel monkey, and kinkajou. Over the years he'd downed fish-eyeball soup, mountain oysters, and raw prairie dog. He could manage roasted monkey and a few bugs, but would pass on the beer two women were making by softening tough cassava stalks with their own saliva and spitting the juice into a bowl to ferment. Derek, the Brit filming the women, looked a little green. Jake bet himself a dollar Derek wouldn't join them for dinner that night.

Mawgis tapped Jake's shoulder. The tiny translator felt loose in Jake's ear. He pushed it back into place.

"Shall we walk among the trees?"

The forest loomed like a presence, something felt as well as seen, lurking just beyond the clearing's edge. Jake inhaled a deep, wet breath. Two steps, four, half a dozen. The spacious camp surrendered to a dense landscape, pulsing with too much color, writhing with too much life. Leaves in a thousand shades of green blocked the sun's light, leaving the forest floor as dim as evening. Orchids in vibrant purples, yellows, and glowing whites clung to trunks and branches of trees so tall Jake couldn't see their tops.

"Walk carefully," Mawgis said.

The ground beneath Jake's boots was spongy. Moisture seeped out of the dark mulch, oozing around his heels with each step. Rainwater fell from the leaves like a second cloudburst, soaking his clothes and making his skin prickle in spite of the heat. He sluiced off the water with his hands as best he could.

Mawgis chuckled under his breath. "By parrot hatching, the water will seem fine to you."

Water dripped from the leaves constantly, even now in the dry season. The bugs were huge, many of them poisonous, and they got into everything. Jake didn't know when parrot hatching might be, and he didn't want to stay long enough to find out. "Make the deal and get out," he'd been told. That was fine by him.

They walked awhile without speaking, Jake following carefully in Mawgis's footsteps along a narrow path that wound through the dense trees. A small green tree frog croaked angrily, leaped from a branch, and seemed to simply disappear. The idle translator hummed in Jake's ear. The monkeys had departed, but the forest rang with the wild cackling of birdcalls.

"Why have you journeyed all this way to see me?" Mawgis asked over his shoulder, not breaking stride.

It seemed an odd question. The Salesians had set up the meeting, given Mawgis the translator, and taught him how to use it. They must have told Mawgis why he was coming.

"I've been asked by the chiefs of many countries and businesses—a society of helpers," Jake said, wondering how else he might describe a humanitarian aid group, "what we call World United, to speak with you about benesha."

Mawgis stopped and turned back to face him. "Benesha? Benesha is just rocks."

Benesha meant "soft fire," according to the Tabna-English dictionary. Ashne Simapole, the head of World United, had said the name was fortuitous, being so close to the English *beneficial* and the Portuguese *benéficio*. The similarity put people in the right frame of mind, he'd said.

"Why do your people want rocks?"

"You and I are men who've been many places and seen many things," Jake said. "There are places in the world where children are too weak from hunger to brush the flies off their faces or even to cry. Every day children and mothers and fathers die because there is not enough to eat. Our scientists have discovered that if animals eat grain mixed with benesha, their meat is more nourishing. A bird that would feed only you and me could, with benesha, feed us and eight more."

Mawgis's tar-colored eyebrows shot up. His eyes went wide. "Ten people can eat one small bird and all will have enough? Such great magic. Your wizards must be strong to have found out this thing."

In truth, it had been mere luck that the mineral's protein-enhancing properties had been discovered. The benesha had originally been fed to mice. The mice were fed to dogs. The dogs didn't get hungry again for a very long time.

"With benesha," Jake said, "everyone can have enough to eat. No child need ever go hungry again. You can make that happen."

"Humph," Mawgis said. He made a quick turn and sped down the faint path that nearly disappeared in the choked tangles of roots and thick layers of decaying leaves.

Jake bolted after him, almost running into him when Mawgis came to a sudden stop. They'd come in a circle. The camp lay a few yards ahead.

"I will think on this," Mawgis said, and moved off faster than Jake could follow, leaving him standing alone in the forest among the oppressive trees.